Black Matilda

Jon Gray Lang

BLACK MATILDA

MachinesoftheInfinitePress.com

Cover Image by Tithi Luadthong

ISBN 978-1-7323305-2-8

Library of Congress Control Number: 2021900709

Jon Gray Lang

To Cindy and Jimmy, I really appreciate everything that you've done for me to help get this undertaking off the ground.

Jon Gray Lang

THE MATILDA SERIES
The Matilda
Twistin' Matilda
Black Matilda
Secret Matilda
Waltzing Matilda

Also by Jon Gray Lang
Nun with a Gun: Town with No Name

one

Be So Happy

"Priority systems booting up... Scanning for damage... external damage only... Run outlying scan... Three humanoids in close proximity... Minor movement... Activation of wetware in progress... Loading... Loading..."

A sudden intake of breath pulled Luli Qing free of her nightmare. But it wasn't a dream. The bars of a small cage truly did press against her chest. As she tried to move, the clank of restraints around her wrists startled her. Shackles bound her ankles, too. Straining to look past the toes of her boots, Luli peered into the area around her in a struggle to get her bearings. She could just make out a dark, cluttered corridor beyond the confines of her cage.

"Come on, brain, focus," she hissed.

"Where in all the hells am I?"

She tugged once more against the manacles until a hum of conversation brought her up short. "Where's that coming from?" she wondered in a whisper.

Looking straight up, she saw a tiny flight deck that lay just above her head. Anguish ripped through her mind as she recognized the three crewmen, "You!" Luli fought against her restraints with renewed strength, "You pricks murdered Vijay!"

"Hey, the pretty shell woke up," chuckled the bulky figure in the center.

The tall one at the nav station slowly rose to his feet and kicked the cage, "I guess we'll have to tranq her again. Pretty damn resilient detox system in that chassis." He opened a small cabinet and floated over, "A double dose, you think?"

"Yeah, Ian, that should do the trick," the last one agreed. "We'll need her under for the next two jump gates. Once we get past those, it won't make a shred of difference. There won't be a soul out there to hear a damn thing she does."

"Where the hell are you taking me?" she screamed.

Laughter broke out amongst the three as the needle punctured the skin along the joint in her neck.

Luli growled, "If you don't let me go, you'll regret it. You all will."

Her voice spiraled off into a moan as the man's head grew larger and his voice dropped a couple of octaves. "What was in tha...?"

***

The lounge on the Matilda rang with voices as Galena hurried to join the meeting already in progress. The room strained with the tension between everyone. But what else could be expected? Luli was missing and the Captain had kicked Barney off the ship. She walked in and took a seat at the large table.

Captain Jacquotte Delahaye nodded as Galena joined them, "Now, tell me again what the staff of Club Meltdown told you."

Frustration edged Anton's voice, "We've been over this a hundred times. The place was packed but it was like any other night. No alarms were triggered. No one saw or heard anything out of the ordinary."

"We went over the green room with a fine-toothed comb," added Derain. "Besides the blood and the lump of Luli's scalp, the only DNA left in the room was Vijay's. They must have used a Mist-Burner to remove all traces of themselves."

"We've got nothing, Jacq," Anton lamented shaking his head slowly.

Jacquie tweaked the bridge of her nose, changing focus toward Galena, "Where are we with Mr. Leon's cargo, Lieutenant?"

"What we've received has all been tied down." Galena answered, "Mr. Leon's contact said the last crates should arrive by tomorrow."

"At least something is going right," muttered Jacquie. Her hands gripped the table, "Do we have anything to go on for Lu? Anything at all?"

Derain brought up his data pad, "One of my contacts came across a news story that could be related. Another deep spacer's body was found in a system on the other side of Consortium controlled space. Her obituary was posted about four months back."

"I'm trying to understand," said Galena, leaning in. "Besides them both being deep spacers, what makes you think they're related?"

"It's what was done to the bodies," he replied. "The skin from both skulls had been cut back to expose the memory cores. Her core was missing, too."

"Great," muttered Anton. "We're after a serial killer."

"We don't know that for sure," Jacquie quipped.

"You weren't there, Jacq! You didn't see what those monsters did to Vijay!" Anton yelled, his throat aching with emotion, "You didn't see how happy she was before she disappeared."

"Don't lose hope," Galena said into the quiet. "If Luli taught me anything, it's don't lose hope."

Anton laughed harshly, "I wonder if we robbed Barney of hope. Maybe Derain's contacts will read about his death next."

Jon Gray Lang

Jacquie seethed with anger, "Don't you dare bring him up!"

Derain knocked on the table interrupting the byplay, "I'll check with my contacts, again. Maybe they'll find something."

Anton kicked himself away from the table, "I can't be anywhere near you, right now Jacq. If you need me, I'll be on the Cyclops." As he marched out of the lounge, the clump of his magnetic boots punctuated the brutal silence.

***

"Systems rebooting... Assessment complete... Connecting..." Luli blinked rapidly as she came to. She kept her breath silent when she rolled over to spy on her captors. There wasn't much to see as they kept their chit-chat light while they went about their assigned tasks.

Her eyes wandered over the antiquated bridge layout. It was a design that tugged at distant memories. A jumble of comm equipment littered the starboard side while the nav console lay wedged against the port bulkhead. The pilot's seat squatted in the dead center of the bridge. Above it hung an old, unused coupling unit. Something about the bow instrumentation struck her as familiar, although she couldn't recall why.

"Hey Franco, we at a safe distance?" the man at the nav console asked as he dialed out the star map on his screen.

Luli stumbled through her sluggish thoughts, '*They said his name before... What was it? Ian?*'

"We're out of comm range of the ring," the man at the comm answered. "The patrol ship is on the backside of the outer planet. I'd say we can make a break for it."

"Good," replied Ian. "Destination endpoint is mapped. Marcus shut down the sub lights."

"They are down and out," answered the pilot. "Cycling the drive now."

A deep thrum vibrated the decking under Luli. She placed her hand against the bulkhead, "This feels familiar..."

Ian's voice broke her reverie, "Quarks are generated. Entangling now."

"Quarks are away," Marcus stated.

"Quarks?" Luli squeaked. "No, it can't be!"

The ship swung hard to port and accelerated away. "Remember, this is a short jump. Cut the link between the two as soon as possible."

"I know how to do my job, Marcus," Ian muttered. "Just be ready to do yours."

Franco chuckled into the tension, "Looks like Ian can't handle a little criticism, eh Marcus?"

"Our end is locked in," Marcus grumbled. "Whenever you're ready... Ian."

Ian gave him the finger and slapped at the switch to cut the connection. In regular space, two quarks escalated away from each other until the tenuous string that connected them snapped. This produced phantom energies that forcibly reformed the connection but only succeeded within the fourth dimension. The two quarks remained in regular space until the string blossomed into a wormhole. When the mouth of it appeared in the bow port, a gasp of recognition escaped Luli.

The wormhole slowly warped in upon itself as it grew larger in open space. Luli felt the decking shudder underneath as the pull of the wormhole reached out for the ship. Gravitational waves buffeted the vessel until it settled within the eye of the storm. The interior of the wormhole twinkled invitingly with reflections from the stars that extended beyond it.

Marcus glanced over his shoulder, "Damn, I think she's awake again. You sure you gave her a double dose?"

"I swear I did," Ian groused. "She must have one hell of a filtering system."

Franco leered as he pointed out the window, "Been a while since you've seen one of those up and close, eh?"

"Leave the cyborg alone," Marcus muttered. "We'll deal with it on the flip side."

"Don't matter either way," Franco chuckled. "Once we're on the Polypheme, she won't see anything ever again." The Demetrius was pulled into the eye and slid its way through.

Luli stared into the heart of the

wormhole and shuddered. She didn't know where they were headed or what they wanted from her. After what they had done to Vijay, the only thing she knew for sure was that the other end only held an open promise of death. "Please Tom, get me a way out of this."

***

Jacquie slumped into the pilot seat with one arm thrown over her head. She was the only one on the bridge. It had been a tough three days and the hangover wasn't helping her think. Neither was the black eye. Mr. Leon's cargo was strapped to the decking and the cargo containers had been locked onto the hull before they lost Luli to Gods-who-knew where or why. She wished Barney was here to help her see a way out of this, but that brought up a completely different mess.

She snarled, "Gods be damned for that day."

He had always been there for her, but at the same time how could he harbor such a dark secret from her? How could he not have known that his mere presence would cost her everything? Betrayal from the one place she would never have expected. The knowledge of it weighed in her heart like a stone.

Anton had torn into her for kicking Barney off the Matilda. It was one of his rare emotionally charged moments when he wasn't being jocular or the fool. The Lieutenant had soundly beaten her for it and she still had the bruises to show for it. Derain had become more distant and the few words they had shared were cold.

But even thinking of Barney reignited her anger. How could he have done this to her? She had trusted him more than anyone. He had been her cornerstone. Because of that, his place in her parent's murder cut that much deeper. The words she'd had with her crew had only seated that anger the more in the dark corners of her soul.

She cursed, "I made my choice and I will deal with the consequences. No matter how painful they may be."

Derain walked past the hatch to the bridge on his way to the hangar. Jacquie called out to him and he stopped in his tracks. His shoulders straightened and his expression deadened as he entered the bridge.

"You called, Captain?" he asked as he came to a standstill in front of her.

Nothing but cold words from him. She received the same from Anton and Galena. In their minds, she deserved it. In hers, it hurt all the more.

She tilted her head as she looked him up and down, but there was no return gaze from him. Her eyes slid to the bow port which brimmed with the darkness of space in the Erebus system. Stars twinkled in the distance as she turned back to him and hid her heart away.

Jon Gray Lang

"I don't like this plan, Derain. Separating us only makes us the weaker."

He brought his eyes level with hers, "It's simple. We don't have any leads and three ships can cover more of Consortium controlled space than one. Split up, we can follow any hint or rumor to its source all the faster." He pursed his lips, "It's not ideal, but there aren't any other workable options on the table. None with a timeline of success, no matter how thin."

"I know, Derain. I even agree with it, fundamentally. I just don't like it."

"Some decisions are foolish, and some are foolhardy. You have to roll with what the hand deals you in the meantime." He stepped back into the hallway, "Now if you'll excuse me, we launch soon, and I still have some prep work to do."

She felt the bite in his words as he disappeared around the bend. Even Derain was getting brusque now. Maybe getting everyone off the ship would help ease tensions. Maybe finding Luli would make everything better. Maybe they would all fail and that would simply be the end of it.

***

Captain Ariel Khan slowly brought her ship, the Copperhead, to as close a relative stop as could be reached in the depth of space. As the ship slowed to a halt, it matched the spin of the latest acquisition of Mr. Leon's enterprise, the

Jon Gray Lang

Independence. The tunnel extended out from the Copperhead and enveloped the airlock of the Independence.

"Not really an acquisition, to be honest. More like contracted out to his enterprise," she muttered under her breath.

The ship's bosun called out, "Tunnel lock is engaged, Captain."

"Thank you, Reynard. Please have someone go collect Mr. Leon."

According to her employer, she was going to meet one of the 'heroes' of the last failed revolution. The woman had survived the bloodbath on Timmony Bay and then was locked away for her crimes against the state. Hero might be a bit of a misnomer, pondered Ariel. "How can anyone come back from that and still be called a hero?"

Mr. Leon came around the corner followed by the Captain's two engineers, Myles and Helena. They carted a med tube between them and it rolled to a stop at the airlock.

"Ah, good day to you Captain," greeted Mr. Leon. "How are you faring?"

"All fine and dandy, Mr. Leon. Though, I do have a quick question. You said we were going to be picking up some cargo from the Independence?"

"That is correct, Captain. I gave the specs to your engineers."

"The hatch is opening, Captain," announced Reynard from the control panel.

Once it fully opened, a battle-hardened woman stood front and center in the tunnel. Her clothing belied anything military but it hung on her muscled frame as if the outfit could only be a uniform. Her eyes were hard and her hair was cut close to the sides of her head. Ariel recognized her as Rosa Keri, one-time freedom fighter, apparently now Commander of the Independence. Two genorgs dressed in Consortium military fatigues came up behind her with their rifles held at the ready. To Ariel, the two genorgs were an anomaly. She hadn't seen anyone decorate a drone to stick out in a crowd, but she could've picked these two out of a sea of them. Both had bizarrely fashioned hair and sported that wolfish look people get when they've seen or done too much and only expected more of the same.

Rosa Keri stood at attention as she stated, "Permission to come aboard, Captain?"

"Permission granted, uh Commander."

Rosa's face broke into a self-deprecating smile, "Only when she's off the ground, Captain. Only when she's off the ground."

The two genorgs slung their rifles over their shoulders and took the med tube from the engineers. Myles and Helena stepped back rather hastily. They watched as the genorg soldiers disappeared down the tunnel with it. Rosa walked onto the Copperhead's deck and strolled over to Captain Khan.

Mr. Leon smiled at them as he headed into the Independence, "Why don't you let the dear Captain know what's going on, Rosa. I have so much to talk about with your crew mates and so little time!" He gave them both a small wave, "Don't wait up for me."

two

Eyes on You

Once Luli regained consciousness, she knew that she was no longer caged on the Demetrius. She found herself in the middle of a poorly lit room that had very light gravity and strange black markings were scratched into the floor. With the constant low rumble for power and life support systems running in the background, she knew she wasn't on a natural planetary body. The walls were heavily pitted, and corrosion laced its way across the only hatch entry she could see. The way the scarring was deeply ingrained into the metal made it seem as if this room had been open to space for decades, if not for centuries. As to what ship or station or where in the known galaxy it was, she had no clue.

As far as she could tell, there was no

Jon Gray Lang

one else in the room with her. But she couldn't escape. Her machine body was locked in the spread-eagled position for repair mode. She tried to bring her arms to her side, but they wouldn't budge. She couldn't bring her legs together either. She strained to get any movement from her chassis, but she wasn't able to even move her fingers.

A male voice whispered from behind her, "Ms. Qing. Please desist. Your cyborg operating system has been compromised and we now have control over your physical form. The shell you exist within will no longer respond to you without a command from me first."

Luli searched around until she spied the small camera mounted in the corner to the left of the hatch. There was another in the corner to the right but this one had something growing around it. She tried to make out what it was, but her mind only processed it as rot.

She tried looking behind her, but her muscles continued to ignore her commands. "There must be cameras in the remaining corners as well." She pushed all of her will into straining against her chassis, hoping for some sign of movement. A small cry of frustration escaped her.

An audible sigh came through the comm, "Shut her down."

Luli gasped as her system was flooded with suppressants. Her vision systems fluttered through their spectrum settings. She could almost swear that a larval creature inhabited the corner near the growths on the wall. As she tried to focus on it, the long arm of somnolence grabbed her and dragged her unwillingly into its embrace.

***

A sliver of light bisected the Matilda's hangar bay. The glow originated from the cockpit of the Cyclops. Anton Roane lay ensconced in the pilot's seat, huddled over the pilot's console. He pulled up the Consortium news and ran a search for stories that mentioned deep spacers. As he waited for it to compile, he kept going back to that night. Vijay's corpse staring up at him with those dead eyes and Luli nowhere to be found.

"Why, though? Why leave his body and take hers?"

His fingers flipped through the days old compiled news reports searching for a lead. The idea was to track down the remaining deep spacers. The others might know who was butchering them for something hidden in their memories. If they didn't, then keep them under surveillance and hope that the killer made a break for one of them. With two of them dead, it had promise.

"It's as thin as flying on empty with a bare hold, but at least it's a plan," sighed Anton in resignation.

He and Derain had pushed the idea to split up to cover more ground. Jacquie had finally relented, even though she didn't like it.

"Sucks for her," growled Anton. "She's made enough shit decisions recently. And if Luli's still alive, she is running out of time." His teeth glinted as he rubbed his hands together, "Besides, I finally have my own ship."

"You wish," muttered a voice behind him.

***

Luli's eyes nearly burst from her head as she woke in shock to the endorphins flooding her system.

"Welcome back, Ms. Qing," proclaimed the voice through the comm. "Do you comprehend your place now?"

"May the Major take you, you bastard!" she cried out.

A dry chuckle filled the room, "There is the spunk that I remember."

"Let me loose and I'll give you a fistful of spunk! Repeatedly!"

The voice murmured disappointedly, "Must this be done the hard way? It is as you wish it then."

Suddenly, Luli's mouth locked closed. No sound escaped her lips. As hard as she tried, no sound came forth. Abruptly, she couldn't blink. Her eyes locked into place and she could feel the air chafe against the orbs as they dried out in the stale air.

The comm clicked back on, "We have control of you, Ms. Qing. We can do this all day, every day until the last of your days. Do you understand?"

Her mouth sprang open and once she realized it, she cursed the voice on the other end of the comm. She cursed the owner of the voice's family and friends, in an unending stream of vitriol and rage.

"Shut her down, please."

***

Captain Kahn invited Rosa to the Copperhead's lounge. On the journey there, Rosa kept her eyes open and took in everything she could from what she was able to see. The vessel was clean and the care in her appearance was important to her Captain and crew.

"You run a tight ship, Captain."

"Yes, I do, and please, call me Ariel," she grinned. "Here we are. May I get you something to drink?"

"Please," responded Rosa, as she wandered over to the table that Ariel had indicated.

Ariel returned with a couple of drinks in hand and set them down on the table. With a deep-seated sigh, the Captain of the Copperhead sat across from her guest. She gazed frankly at Rosa, "Don't take this the wrong way, but I expected you to be taller."

Rosa snorted in response, "I used to get that a lot. Not so much nowadays. You, on the other hand, look exactly as I expected. Competent, strong, with a no-nonsense attitude. I think I could like you, Ariel."

Ariel laughed back, "I think the same of you too, Rosa." She took a sip from her glass. "Since you seem to know the plan, any idea how long he'll be?"

Rosa took a sip of the fragrant liquor and her eyebrows shot up, "This is bleeding fantastic. Color me surprised."

Ariel admired the amber liquid through the glass, "It was a gift I received from another Captain. Captain Delahaye. Have you heard of her?"

Rosa raised her glass to cover her mouth as she choked, "We've run into each other before." She kept the glass in her hand, "About Mr. Leon, he shouldn't be more than a couple of hours. While genorgs may not be the greatest conversationalists, they do make decisions relatively quickly."

"I could only imagine. Any idea what we're bringing on board my boat?" Ariel asked as she took another sip.

Rosa carefully set the glass down on the table, "I do know what your cargo is, Captain." Her hands settled into fists, "You'll be shipping and selling genorgs into servitude."

Ariel spat out her whiskey in surprise.

Rosa whispered into the silence, "I feel the same way."

three

Sail On

Galena watched from the airlock window as Derain flew the Waratah out of the hangar, followed shortly by Anton in the Cyclops. She stood there until the hangar bay doors clanged shut. "Such a strange sensation. I feel... I feel I will miss them almost as much as Luli..."

Deep in thought, she crossed her arms over her chest as she made her way back to the lounge. With Barney kicked off the ship, that left just Jacquie and herself on the Matilda and she was simply too large a vessel to be handled by a crew of one. Galena snorted at something Barney had said, "Only a madman would try to fly a ship this big alone."

As much as Jacquie might want that right now, she couldn't do it. Derain had his ship to fly and Anton refused to forgive Jacquie. He was still angry with her for sending Barney out alone. In fact, his last words had been that he would make her change her mind if it was the last thing he did. Derain had kept silent during this outburst, but he edged up behind Anton to throw his support behind him. So, they had decided to leave before Jacquie could kick them off. That meant she was left to pick up the pieces of her Captain.

Galena uncrossed her arms and bared her teeth in an unsettling grin, "That's going to be more than enough work for this trip."

As she entered the lounge, her hands ran along the surface of Luli's ukulele. The tiny instrument was ancient, but the newly filled crack almost blended in with the grain of the old wood. After it had been released from police evidence, Anton had repaired it and then hung it in the lounge. What had he said again? Oh yes, "Let this stand as a promise that we will find Luli at any cost."

Jacquie's voice came over the lounge comm, "Lieutenant? We're coming up on the jump gate, I'll need you on comm."

"On my way, Captain." She looked back wistfully before she stepped out of the lounge and hurried her way to the bridge. "Becoming human is more painful than I had imagined."

***

Luli's eyelids fluttered open and a

shuddering breath escaped her as the endorphins pushed her to wakefulness. Her head moved with ease and she took full advantage of it before trying anything else. After a quick look around, she amended her initial thoughts about her surroundings when she spotted a couple cameras in the remaining two corners of the room. What she hadn't expected was the grime streaked one-way mirror on the opposing wall from the hatch. Her eyes tracked to the comm speaker mounted above the mirror.

"Has the lesson been learned, Ms. Qing?"

She nodded slowly while keeping an eye out for any movement. But there was nothing. No lights or shadows shown in the one-way mirror. The room on the other side might be occupied or it might not. Her eyes widened as her arms fell to her side of their own volition. Her knees unlocked and she had to catch herself as she crashed onto the decking.

"We will see if the lesson has taken," came from the speaker.

Luli pulled herself up and stretched out her legs. She proceeded to stretch her arms as she glanced over to the one-sided mirror. "Thank you. I... I apologize for my misunderstanding. My memories of the last few hours have been spotty and very emotional to me." She stopped stretching and her hands came together in a clasp, "Tell me, does Vijay live?"

There was a long pause and only light

static came through the comm. "The shell that housed what you knew as Vijay Bhatti was broken. The entity known as Vijay has been freed from its cage to return home. There is no need to be sad over the loss of the body as this is the most fortunate of circumstances."

Luli gulped and the sides of her face grew taut as she tried to stop the tears from forming. She began to choke from the pressure until finally, she couldn't hold back a long shuddering moan. She hugged her arms to herself and began walking around the center of the room... around and around, she went.

"Thank you for letting me know. I... I appreciate it very much." She paused in the middle of the room and asked, "Would it be possible to have a chair brought in for me? I mean, I know I don't have to sit, but it is a human thing that I feel the need for from time to time."

"That can be arranged. Thank you for your coopera..."

Luli turned and sprinted directly toward the mirror. As she leaped to clear the lower wall, her entire body went stiff. She crashed through the mirror and landed between two of the men she recognized from the night Vijay was killed. Hot, angry tears spilled from her eyes before her tear ducts were shut off by the mysterious owner of the voice. Her eyelids clamped closed and she struggled with her body as she was chemically dragged to the brink of unconsciousness.

Jon Gray Lang

"The lesson is still unlearned," the voice growled in annoyance.

***

Anton watched from the Cyclops as the Waratah disappeared through the gate. Shortly afterward, the Matilda slipped through on her separate journey. He fidgeted in the seat for a moment before he gave up and slumped into it.

"Stupid seat. You can come out now," Anton grumbled. "Where in Consortium space are we headed again?"

Barney fussed about in the back of the small ship, "It's weird to watch her leave. Weird without me on it. You know, I'm not sure I've ever seen her go through a gate from the outside."

"I bet it is. By the way, you look ridiculous in that priest robe," laughed Anton.

Barney grumbled as he pulled at the garment, "I feel ridiculous. Hell, I feel like I'm going to be struck down for even being in this getup. This is full-on blasphemy to my people, you know."

Anton smirked, "But it's a perfect cover story. No one will question a Titan in that thing on a ship like this. Well, another Titan might, but I've now seen a total of three, and two of them are dead."

Anton turned back to the nav console, "Where are we headed again?"

Barney's eyes widened as he stomped

over, "You haven't entered the coordinates yet? We're almost to the front of the gate line! Gods! Set it for the Prima-Sotra system."

"Uh, the Prima-Saucer?"

"Prima-Sotra. Get back over there, I'll do it," Barney harrumphed.

Anton laughed as he slid out of the way. Barney typed furiously into the nav computer and glared at him with a vengeance.

Barney admonished him, "We're going to Reverie Station."

"Oh, that's right..." Anton exclaimed.

"The last known sighting of Yannick Specht, squeezebox player, and one-time deep spacer," they said in unison.

four

Darkness

The Waratah, the somewhat more worse-for-the-wear troop transport, plowed through the fifth jump gate on its journey and shot into the wormhole. It would take about an hour before the ship came through the other side into the Aken system. There was very little to do in the meantime except sit back and wait for the trip to come to an end.

Going back home. It wasn't something that Derain had thought would happen any time soon if ever, to be honest. But there it was. There was nothing but rivalry to be found there, nothing but altercations both physical and verbal.

His father's last words when he slammed the door in his face, "If you ever come back here bringing trouble, I will beat it out of you and leave you for dead!"

"Only grandfather watched out for me after that and he was already an old man..." Derain muttered, "Not in the books for me to go back. I swore I never would, but here I am on the way. Damn the luck."

One of his informants had come across a flight itinerary for the deep spacer, Bartolo Tufaro. He was set to perform a show on Derain's home world of Aketi in less than a week's time.

It made the most sense for him to be the one to go. He knew the place better than the rest of the crew. Never mind that he knew the bad parts of the main city better than most of the inhabitants on the planet. Besides, it might be good to see how the family was doing. It had been a long time. He was willing to bury the hatchet if they were.

"One minute until entry into the Aken system. Please display your ident or be fired upon," crackled through the ship's comm.

His left eyebrow quirked up at that. The Consortium seemed to be taking more of an iron fist approach to the rules recently. The Waratah broke through the ring and he keyed in the ident. It took a minute, but after he was cleared for system entry, he set course for Aketi. Another two days until arrival. He stared out the bow port and could barely make out the pinprick that was home.

"Gods, I hate this system."

Jon Gray Lang

***

"I repeat, Cyclops, please explain your purpose for entering our space," came through the comm.

"That's you, Barney." Anton grinned wickedly. "Explain to the Reverie Station tower what a Titan Retrieval team is doing here. Oh, and sound convincing."

"Shush you," Barney shot back.

He keyed the comm over to the tower channel and waited for the video feed to connect. As his presence in the priestly robes appeared on the camera, the tower representative took on a more respectful tone.

"Excuse me, dignitary. Would you please be able to provide a reason for needing entry at Reverie Station?"

Barney sized the fellow up, "Of course. We have come to your fine station to play games of chance and so forth."

Anton whispered, "I think you're being too polite... "

Barney glared at him from the corner of his eye as he continued, "So could we please expedite this process? My time is important, and I have precious little of it to waste."

Anton grinned at Barney, "Better."

The tower representative grew flustered and keyed through multiple commands on his screen. "Of course, of course, dignitary. My apologies for the delay. You have been granted entry. Please proceed to Hangar Bay Meridian, slot 1812. Once again, my apologies for the delay."

Barney threw on a sardonic grin, "Apology accepted." He disconnected the comm and glared at Anton, "Fly the ship, pilot, and be quick about it!"

"Sir, yes sir," Anton laughed as he took the Cyclops into the landing bay and searched for their numbered slot.

He brought the ship in and locked it into the landing skid, "Alright mighty leader. What's our next move?"

"Getting me out of this ridiculous get-up," he cursed as he struggled to remove the robe.

With a deep-seated sigh of relief, he threw the robe onto the carpeted floor of the yacht. His joints popped as he stretched. Absentmindedly, he scratched at himself before he noticed Anton waiting with feigned bated breath for his next command.

"Fine. The next thing we do is to find this guy and see if he knows anything." Once Anton unbuckled his seat restraint, he stepped back into the light gravity of the ship. "Well? Let's get a move on. No time like right this bloody minute."

"Of course, your eminence. My apologies for making you wait."

"Oh, shut up, Anton," grumbled Barney.

Jon Gray Lang

⁎⁎⁎

Rosa sat perched on top of a crate in the cargo bay of the Copperhead. She idly kept an eye on Captain Kahn as the woman paced angrily back and forth waiting for Mr. Leon's return. Ariel hadn't taken the news of her new cargo well.

Rosa understood her anger. There were stories and rumors aplenty of the horrible living conditions on the ships that carted drones across Consortium space and sold them into servitude. Genorgs had been designed to handle living conditions that a natural-born would find nigh unlivable. A crew could make a lot of currency if they cut costs that would keep a genorg at top condition. Food, water, and air were only needed in the minority and if some of the cargo died, well then only a portion of the profit margin was hurt.

Rosa had felt sick to her stomach when she had learned the fate of the crew of the Independence. Never mind how her involvement in the whole business affected her sense of self-worth. The more she had come to learn about Mr. Leon's business plans; the more she wished she had rethought her choice. In the end, she still knew she would've chosen to live. The worst part was trying to understand how he planned to convince the genorgs to voluntarily give up their freedom.

Ariel stopped pacing and stared daggers down the airlock tunnel. The focus of her anger stepped into the cargo bay followed by about a hundred genorgs, each one armed to the teeth. Omega immediately started delegating locations in the cargo bay and the genorgs began to bivouac the area. Everything was very orderly, and Ariel stood in the middle of it like a rock. Rosa just shook her head. Somehow the bastard had convinced them to sell their freedom.

"Mr. Leon!" shouted Captain Kahn. "A word please."

He smiled as he replied to her, "Of course."

He followed her into a corner of the cargo bay, but Omega hung back discreetly. Captain Kahn spied Omega standing off to the side and waved her over. Mr. Leon stared blithely around as if his mind were elsewhere.

Once Omega joined them, Ariel immediately lit into the man, "I refuse to do this, Mr. Leon. I'm not turning my ship into a... a slaver! Go ahead and break my contract. Make it impossible for me and my crew to find work again, but I am not going to be a party to this."

Mr. Leon crossed his arms and checked his fingernails for dirt, "Captain... Captain... slaver is such an antiquated term. I would never allow you and your crew to be called such a thing. Please keep in mind that these drones aren't remotely considered human. The Consortium considers them goods to be bought and sold, no different from a sack of grain." He turned to

Omega, "No offense."

"No offense is taken," Omega stonily replied.

Captain Kahn continued, "I can't sink my ship to this... this level. Once you go down that route, you carry that stink with you forever."

"Oh, I've already covered that," replied Mr. Leon. "I've had a separate name registered for this vessel for this and all future deliveries of the same sort. Your hands will be metaphorically clean. Omega here will oversee the sales. You'll be in command except when we're at a port for these sorts of deliveries. And we should get a move on as we have many ports of call to make."

Ariel looked back from Mr. Leon in consternation to Omega in complete confusion, "How could you do this to your own kind?"

"It is the will and the way," replied Omega. "Now, if you'll excuse me, Captain." She marched back to her sisters and assisted them in getting placed in their berths.

Ariel just stared at Omega's retreating back, "What did you say to get them to go along with this?"

Mr. Leon's expression took on a strange cast, "Oh, even a drone understands the needs of the business and all that rigmarole."

five

La Vie En Rose

"There you are," Jacquie said as she walked into the upper deck airlock prep room.

Galena was crammed into a corner of the chamber. Most of the spacesuits had been dragged off their hangers and the Lieutenant had buried herself under the pile. It seemed as if she were hiding from something.

"Are you hiding from something? You're getting pretty good at it if you are."

Galena peeked around an armored spacesuit leg, "What am I doing here?"

Jacquie smiled as she moved some of the pile out of the way, "I was wondering the same thing. This isn't the first time I've found you hidden away."

Galena blinked, "I... I have no

recollection   of other times."

Jacquie picked up one of the suits and rehung it, "To be honest, sometimes when I find you, you scare the shit out of me. It's like you're having a conversation with someone I can't see. Or being interrogated. It changes. I can't explain it."

"I haven't felt right since Luli pulled me off the Avadora," Galena murmured. "Sometimes it feels like I am dreaming and something else has control of me. Other times, I find myself in parts of the ship and I don't know how I got there."

"Like now?"

Galena nodded but then her eyes grew unfocused. "Are we the same?" she whispered.

The muscles in Galena's body seized and then became rigid. Her breathing became labored and she shook as if from tremors of a seizure. Screams tore past the genorg's lips. It was horrifying to hear and frightening to see. Jacquie fell to her knees and tried to keep Galena from hurting herself. She grabbed both wrists and straddled the Lieutenant, pinning her to the decking.

"Wake up!" the Captain shouted. "Wake up, Galena! Please, wake up!"

As suddenly as the seizure had started, it stopped. Galena's eyes cracked open and only darkness stared back at Jacquie. The pressure on her mind made Jacquie slam her eyes shut to break contact. After a moment, Galena's body relaxed, and Jacquie looked down to see her eyes wide open and red from fear.

"Am I still here? Or is this the dream?" Galena gasped before her eyes rolled into the back of her head and she passed out.

Jacquie bit her lip, "I hope you're here with me. I really hope so."

***

Barney glanced up from a recessed doorway when a ruckus down at the end of the hall made its presence known.

"It's not my fault!" Anton shouted as he sprinted past. He disappeared down another passageway with a mob screaming bloody murder was on his tail. Barney shook his head in consternation.

Anton went back over the last hour on Reverie Station. It had all started out so innocently. The gaming parlor had been packed and working the crowd for rumors about the deep spacer had been a breeze. No one on the station was concerned about his possible disappearance. Some of the players said they'd seen Yannick as recently as yesterday. Others said not since he landed over a week ago. A cardsharp had mentioned offhandedly that the ship Yannick had arrived on was looking for a replacement now, but the scuttlebutt was he was looking to stay on and was shopping his options. There was definitely something shady going on and that was exactly the kind of lead they were looking for.

Then everything went south with a vengeance. Sure, he had been cheating a little, but nothing too obvious. Anton was surprised that anyone bothered to notice.

"I should have known when to quit," Anton huffed between strides. "If there is one thing a loser looks for it's a chance to bad-mouth the winner."

Yes, that last trick had been sloppy on his part, but still, why should he be blamed for their poor playing? Anton clicked his comm, "Uh Barney? Look, I know this looks bad, but I've got good news of a sort. I'm forwarding everything I have to you. Anton out."

Anton looked over his shoulder, "Now I just need a place to hide and bide my time."

***

"... I'm forwarding everything I have to you. Anton out," came through Barney's comm.

Barney listened intently when more of the mob tore past. He shook his head again. The fool was going to get himself caught, beaten, and left for dead... again.

"Every time I think you've learned your lesson, you go and prove me wrong." Information began to stream across Barney's data pad, "But you do come through in the pinch, don't you. Slot 2258? Well now, that's pretty close. Think

I'll go ask his old shipmates a few questions."

Barney waited for a break in the crowd and headed toward the berth of Yannick's old ship, the Lagos. It was a good sign that a body hadn't been found yet. That meant there was still a chance that the deep spacer was alive and kicking somewhere out there.

"That's another point to take into consideration," Barney speculated. "If he is still alive, he has to be eating, drinking, or whatnot; at least breathing."

He stopped in his tracks. "Oxygen usage." If Yannick was hiding or trapped aboard another ship, the draw on the oxygen usage would be noticeably higher. The station would track and tax the hell out of that. He started walking again and hummed to himself; more options to be on the lookout for.

***

Something was very wrong.

Derain's old neighborhood on Aketi was eerily quiet. Strips of police tape caught on the tufts of tall grass and littered the front yard of his grandfather's home. The windows were boarded up and it looked as if it had been that way for weeks. His brother's house had been the same.

Not a soul had come down the street that ran past the front of his grandfather's house in the past few minutes. "No time like the present,"

Derain muttered as he straightened his coat and walked over to the front door. His elbow smacked through the decorative glass. As it tinkled to the ground, he reached in and turned the handle. The door opened slowly, and he slipped in.

An unused roll of police tape coated in a thin layer of dust perched on the table near the front door. Beyond that, the entire place was a wreck. Drawers had been pulled out of chests, cabinets lay open and their contents were strewn across the floor. It was the same in every room on the main floor and it wasn't any different on the upper floor. Books had been tossed onto the crimson carpet of the small library that his grandfather Mullion had painstakingly put together.

Books. Derain's love of books had been spurred by his grandfather's collection. His great grandfather, Derain Tiwi senior, had come across a myriad of different items working as a salvager, but books, paper books, were something that he had prized especially. He had passed that love down to his son, and he to his grandson.

Nostalgia hit the bounty hunter hard as he bent down to pick one up. The Rubàiyàt by Omar Khayyam, one of his namesake's favorites. A pressing sense of need overtook him and he dug through the pile of books on the floor until he unearthed The Prince by Niccolò Machiavelli and finally The Divine Comedy by Dante Alighieri. He brushed at the dust on the covers and carefully slipped them into the pockets of his long coat.

When he stepped out of the house, he closed the door behind him and stared hard at his reflection. "Do the job first, then find out what happened here."

He turned and his footsteps carried him toward the office of the local constabulary.

Jon Gray Lang

six

Screaming in Digital

The Matilda cruised up to the docking port and waited for the clamps to bring her in. The delay in the hunt for Luli ate at Jacquie, but other things took precedence. "I just need to get Mr. Leon's delivery off my ship then I can search for her."

The shipping manifest pointed to the space station held in the planetary grip of Toros Colony. The star system, designated as DV2665, was a recent discovery. The system was new enough that even though the jump gate was functioning, there were still work crews scattered along the ring scaffolding to complete its build.

Jacquie shut the ship's systems down. Galena had already headed down to the main shaft to unclip the shipping containers from the hull. The

Loading Union out here was surprisingly quick to take their cargo since it contained survival goods for this rock. Jacquie waited down in the cargo bay until Galena joined her.

"Ready to close out this delivery?"

Once Jacquie received the small nod, she waved Galena ahead of her and they both stepped out into the station proper. The dock was dingy, but then the station served as the vacation spot for the miners down below.

Toros Colony was located on a barren dirtball that lacked a breathable atmosphere and had little to offer scenically speaking. But what it did have in spades was resources. That little rock was rich in metals, minerals, and easily convertible fuel sources. The miners who chose to work on this rock would walk away rich. That is if they lived long enough to retire.

Rockfalls were common. Some were rumored to be man-made, but they were still common enough not to be questioned. If your breather slipped down there, you'd suffocate. If you tore your suit, you'd suffocate. Toros was a cruel master, but the rewards could be substantial. If you survived the planet, then you just had to survive the station next.

DV2665.1 Station was a common sight for anyone who had ever been to a mining colony. She was a floating den of iniquity. Every vice that could fleece a miner of their mazuma was here and this included murder. It was a regular cesspool of dross and moral pollution.

The Captain and the Lieutenant traversed the station, bypassing all the hallmarks of a miner's facade of paradise. They both knew the sooner their cargo haul was signed off on and cleared, the sooner they could chart their next step. Luckily for them, rumors and hints flew around like leaves in the wind in a wretched place like this. All you had to do was brave the breeze and listen.

Arriving at the station delivery desk, Jacquie provided the ship's ident with the cargo manifest. It was a matter of moments before everything had been signed and the delivery glowed as completed on her data pad.

"Your payment includes a refueling, Captain," mentioned the associate behind the counter. "Would you like this to be taken care of immediately?"

"Please. That would be wonderful."

The woman scrolled through her screen prompts and clicked the last one with finality, "Your ship refueling should be completed by the morning. Were you looking for a shipment to take? We have a few on the table."

"Can you dump them to my data pad and I'll peruse them later?" asked Jacquie. "I'm not entirely sure where I'm heading to next."

"Of course. Click here, then here. Thank you." The associate scrolled through another screen, "Just so you are aware, the application for delivery acceptance is down, so you'll have to come back here to finalize the process."

"Got it and I've got the list," stated Jacquie. "What's the best and the worst watering hole on this station, if you get my drift?"

The woman stopped what she was doing and gave Jacquie a conspiratorial look, "If you're looking for cheap entertainment, check out the Temptation. If you want, um, questionable entertainment, check out the Nine Lives. By the way, it's lady's night at the Nine Lives."

Jacquie winked in understanding, "They have a problem with genorgs?"

"Drones? Hell, more than half the miners these days are drones. Their mazuma is as good as any." The associate smirked, "... have a problem with genorgs. Been a while since you've been to a mining colony, Captain?"

"Oh yeah, it's been a while. Thanks for the info."

The two women stepped away from the counter and hurriedly moved off. Galena looked around as Jacquie did a quick scan of the shipping options on the table. They continued on in silence until Jacquie swiped the data pad off and put it away.

Galena turned to her, "It's funny. This place seemed vaguely familiar and I didn't know why until I saw them."

She pointed down the hall to a cluster of genorgs that were chained together. They were led forcefully into the space elevator entrance in the center of the station. Many of them were quite young, but all of them had the same confused and lost expression on their faces. As they disappeared around a corner, Galena's arm dropped to her side.

"I have done that walk, Captain. I'm sure I wore that same look with no idea what was going to happen next." Her eyes bored into Jacquie, "Being a miner is a tough life. At least they let them up here sometimes."

Jacquie squirreled away that bit of information. Galena was a quiet one most of the time and rarely shared a story. As they rounded the corner, the sign for the Temptation lit up the area.

"Would you like to join me for a drink, Lieutenant? I'm sure I owe you one from somewhere."

***

"Bring her back slowly, gentlemen."

Luli's eyes fluttered open, but they remained unfocused. Gradually her pupils constricted, and they began to respond to the bright light. Groggily she came to and tried to place her hands in front of the light, but her arms wouldn't move.

"Why so bright?" she mumbled through clenched teeth.

"Welcome back, Ms. Qing." The voice from the comm echoed in the small room, "You may turn the light down, gentlemen."

Luli quieted once she realized she was

still here, wherever here was, and she wasn't alone. The owner of that voice still had a grip on her, whoever it was. The rickety chair she was seated on creaked. Her wrists were manacled to the surface of a beat-up old desk. She tried to wiggle her fingers, but they wouldn't move. The light slowly dimmed, and she was able to see through the broken one-way mirror. Two of her abductors sat behind the shards and operated a control board.

She snarled into the silence, "A control board for me."

"Quite right, Ms. Qing. Quite right." There was a pause that was filled with a light static before it continued, "These are my extra hands, as it were. They do my bidding as I lead them forward to the light that you, yourself, shirk from. Does this make sense to you?"

Luli watched the two men for any change of expression regarding the strange statement, but they remained impassive. "I can honestly say I have no idea what you're talking about."

Franco smirked at her response while Ian nodded slowly. They seemed to make eye contact with something or someone past her shoulder. She couldn't move her head and fear slowly seeped into her belly.

"Now Ms. Qing, may I call you Luli?"

She tried to open her mouth, but her teeth locked in place with a click.

"No matter. We have a

communication problem that must be rectified. You have failed to work with me within the boundaries that we have set. Yet I have met your demands and provided a chair for you as requested. But still, you continue to act rashly. I have neither the time nor the inclination to continue in this vein. The Masters have devised a new lesson for you and hopefully, it will be the last one needed."

Luli felt a hand on her shoulder and then the man she recognized as Marcus came around to her side. He roughly grabbed one of her hands by the wrist. The sensation of his hand encircling her wrist surprised her. She then realized that she was able to flex her fingers and alarms began going off in her head.

"Ms. Qing... Luli... You must understand that we control you. We have complete control of you and there is nothing you can do about that. Once we have that established, then we can move forward in our relationship." There was a long pause, "Is that so much to ask?"

Luli watched as Marcus gripped the middle finger of her left hand and his eyes slid to catch hers in a stare.

"What is happening? What are you going to do? What do you want from me?" The words flew out of Luli in a torrent, but they were only met with silence.

The male voice echoed through the room, "Besides your lovely singing voice, what would you consider the most human feature remaining to you? The process your body went through to become a deep space pilot changed you. All the augments and reinforcements of your joints made you less than human, but also more. However, your hands were left as they were. They are your hands, the very ones that you were born with. Are they not the hands that you play music with in the silent hours of the day? We shut off the control impulses from your hardware, but sadly that lesson did not take. A more permanent lesson is needed."

Marcus tightened his grip on her middle finger and pulled upward. There was a sharp report as the finger bone snapped. Luli tried to scream in pain, but she had no control over her throat. Marcus left that finger pointing skyward and moved to the index finger.

With practiced ease, he bent that one back and it snapped in his grip. He let go and moved on to the pinky finger and the snap of it echoed in her ears. No sound escaped as she couldn't cry out. She could only watch as he methodically went through the fingers on her left hand and broke each one.

"Trapped. I am trapped in my own body and I can do nothing!" the voice in her head wailed.

Her breath came out in ragged gasps and her face was stretched taut from the pain, but she still couldn't scream. The only other sound in the room was the pop of her fingers as they were broken.

She couldn't pull her eyes away from the sight of her mangled fingers. Her breaths came out quick and fast as Marcus reached for the index finger of her right hand. It was the only unbroken finger left. Its sickening snap was the last sound in the room, but it lingered for a long time.

Marcus released her wrists and stepped away from the table. She could barely make him out from the corner of her eye. Suddenly her eyes gushed with hot tears and wails of anguish poured from her throat. Her neck was no longer locked in place. She stared around the room like an animal trapped in a cage. Her eyes clamped shut as sobs shuddered from her chest. She curled into as much of a fetal position as she was able while still being tied to the chair.

She began rocking while whimpering, "What do you want from me? Why are you doing this? Why? Why? Why?"

The voice clicked back over the comm, "Your fingers will never touch the strings of your precious instrument in the same way again. The lesson can continue until you fully understand that you are powerless." There was a long pause before he asked, "Now do you understand, Ms. Qing?"

She nodded in a rush repeatedly, emphatically. Her face was clenched in pain and fear etched itself into the hollows. But deep down there guttered a tiny flame of rage.

Jon Gray Lang

seven

These Boots

Derain stepped into the police station in the biggest city of the backwater planet Aketi. His great grandfather's books, which were crammed inside the pockets of his jacket, slapped against his side when he stopped briefly in the lobby of the station to get his bearings.

The place was still a disaster. Garbage poured out of two trash cans and the windows had a thick layer of grime he didn't think was physically possible. The uniforms behind the glass at the main counter all had that blank stare of being numb to other people's problems. The citizens in line to the counter carried themselves like they needed to yell at someone, and it didn't matter who. In other words, it was a regular day here. Derain cursed until he spotted an officer with his

Jon Gray Lang

arms loaded down with files walking toward the back door.

"Excuse me, sir. Hey!" Derain shouted as he chased the man down.

The officer turned around and he looked strikingly familiar with his tight curly hair and high cheekbones. The officer's expression changed from annoyance to confusion until it softened with recognition.

"Derain? Derain Tiwi? Has the prodigal bastard returned home?"

Derain's mouth opened in shock, "Mmeli? Thando Mmeli? You old cobber, that you?"

The officer nodded and his face lit up with a smile.

"Man, you look like shit! Time has not been kind to you," Derain stated matter of factly.

"I could say the same, but you spacer trash never seem to age." Thando threw up his hand for a high five, "How long has it been?"

Derain's hand slapped Thando's. "You know that time dilation thing. It's hard to tell for us spacer trash."

"It's been at least a couple decades, if not longer." Mmeli turned back to the door and opened it. "Come on over to my desk and we can talk some more. I've got to get these done today," he grumbled as he indicated the folders in his hand.

Derain held the door open and

followed him through. "I didn't think traffic cops had paperwork."

Thando threw a wicked grin over his shoulder, "I'm a detective."

"Oh! Congrats, mate."

Detective Mmeli moved around the corner of his desk and flopped into the chair. He dropped the pile of flimsies into his 'In' basket and motioned Derain to the chair against the side of the desk.

"I've been a detective for years. In fact, I'm a chief inspector now. So, take that, ya mug."

"Sorry, sir. My apologies, sir." Derain threw him a sloppy salute as he settled into the back of the chair. "It's good to see you. Anyone else from the old neighborhood suffering from a strong sense of self-importance?"

"Ha. Ha. Always the funny man. Let's see. Last time I saw you, you brought in a collar and she had smashed your face up pretty well. You're looking alright now, though. You finally get that right block working for you?"

"Point and set."

"Vania was out here looking for you a year ago but she left quick. The usual bunch are still doing just enough to ride on the edge of keeping them out of trouble." The detective's expression changed to one of sadness, "I should have expected you to come out, but I didn't think it would be this soon. You here for the funeral?"

Jon Gray Lang

"Who's gone and died?" Derain smirked. "Actually, hold on that. I'm tracking Bartolo Tufaro. You have anything on him?"

"Are you sure?"

"I'm on a deadline, mate," answered Derain as he pulled out his data pad. "The dead aren't going anywhere. They can wait another minute."

"Oh," Thando muttered in mild shock. "I've only got bad news for you then. His body was discovered in an alley dumpster a couple weeks ago. Someone had done a number on him before they left. Did he skip on bail from some inner world?"

"Nothing like that. He had intel on some perps that I've been tracking," responded Derain. "I was hoping to collect on that. His death kind of screws that source. Do you have his personal effects or his cadaver?"

"We still have him on ice. Did you want to take a look?"

"Yeah. That would be beaut'," Derain replied. "He might have something on him that will point me in the right direction."

"Okay." Detective Mmeli stood up and waved Derain to follow him, "I, uh, have something else to show you down there too."

***

Barney walked back from his meeting

with the Captain of the Lagos. Yannick Specht had disappeared without a word to the crew the second day they had been in port. His crew waited for about a week before starting the search for a new pilot. Time is mazuma and mazuma keeps you burning time, as they say.

He hadn't heard back from Anton, but that wasn't surprising. As much trouble as that man got into, he was usually able to extricate himself without too much hassle. Sometimes he was a little worse for wear, but generally not broken. Barney stopped and studied the color bar map on the station wall. He grunted and headed off toward the port office. Time could be running faster wherever Luli was.

"Hints and rumors aren't getting me anywhere." His hands clenched into fists and he became deadly serious, "Let's see who I need to bribe, break or screw to get a lead."

***

Anton watched from his hiding spot as the mob continued on past down the station hallway. Just to be safe, he waited a few minutes longer, but they didn't come back. He slowly extricated himself from the ventilation shaft and replaced the grate.

"No time like this very moment to get a move on."

He strolled nonchalantly into the

hallway traffic and did his best to blend in. His luck may have gone bad by stirring up that hornet's nest in the gaming parlor, but one young lady had said Specht was supposed to have a show at the local watering hole, the Eclipse. It wasn't much to go on but it wasn't too far away. Maybe he could poke a hornets' nest there, too.

The Eclipse was pretty quiet no matter how hard the lights told you otherwise. If this was the club where a deep spacer was supposed to be performing, it wasn't tonight. The people inside had that look of regulars with a few merchant crews sprinkled in, but everyone kept to their little groups. Anton sidled up to the bar and ordered a whiskey.

"Hey barkeep, I heard that Yannick Specht was supposed to play here tonight." Anton indicated the bar, "This place looks dead."

The bartender sneered, "He was supposed to play a couple nights ago, but the creep bolted halfway through the show."

"He just walked off stage and disappeared?"

"Naw. He should've come out and done at least one encore, but he just rolled out. He didn't even stay to collect his cut of the profits for the evening."

Anton queried, "Wait, he just left? He did the show for free? That's weird."

The bartender stopped for a moment, "Yeah. That is kind of weird. But deep spacers, they don't make a lot of sense. That guy wanted the cheapest vodka we had in the house."

"Them and their sense of self-inflated personality," Anton rolled his eyes.

The barkeep laughed, "I know, right? Anyway, Meg over there can tell you more. She dealt with the skip personally."

"Thanks, I'll ask her. Mind pouring me another round?"

"No problem. Hold on."

Anton glanced over his shoulder at the woman the bartender had pointed out. Meg was, at a guess, somewhere in her twenties or thirties. She had shoulder-length, brown wavy hair that shown lustrous in the overhead lights. Her dark complexion caught the light and gave her an otherworldly glow. Her piercing eyes cut through her face and they seemed to dance with a smile that burst forth from her lips before it disappeared.

"Here you go."

"Thanks."

Anton dropped some mazuma on the bar before he headed off toward Meg and her group of admirers. She stood in the middle of a gaggle of folk that hung on her every word. Anton hung back until there was a break in the conversation.

"You wouldn't happen to be Meg, would you?" he asked as he stepped forward.

She looked him up and down, "Depends on who's asking. Should I know you?"

Anton chuckled a little bit, "Uh,

probably not." As she began to turn away he added, "But you should know the person I represent."

She turned back to face him, quirked an eyebrow, and waited.

"Oh yes. I represent Luli Qing. She's a deep..."

"I know who and what she is. Why should I believe that you know her?"

"I've flown with her for many a year. Anyway, I'm here to..."

She glared at him. "You aren't the first hack this week to tell me that you represent one of the spacers. The last three guys came in saying they represented Bartolo Tufaro. I give them the time of day and then I'm out one Yannick Specht. Trust isn't high on the list today."

"Three men, you say? Could you tell me something about...?"

"You have one minute to say your piece." She continued to glare at him.

A little flustered, Anton jumped in, "Well, um, I'm actually looking for those men you're talking about. They've been misrepresenting themselves and I'm trying to put a stop to..."

Meg looked over her shoulder and nodded at the bouncer. "Time's up. Those creeps are still on the station last I heard." She took the drink from his hand and moued into his face, "Time to go, sailor."

Anton felt a hand grab his shoulder and yank him off his feet. The last thing he saw was

Jon Gray Lang

Meg laughing before another hand grabbed the back of his neck. The bouncer yanked him by the collar and dragged him to the club's doorway.

As he threw him in the hall, the bouncer growled, "Idiot had too much to drink."

eight

More Whisky

Navigation Officer Grissom cleared through the multiple screens open at his station and zeroed in on the arrival beacon. He glanced up and the outer edge of the jump gate appeared at the end of the constructed wormhole. He slowly counted to himself until the ship, the M33, breached the jump gate. The wormhole dissipated behind the vessel.

"We have entered the Erebus system, Captain. Should I set course for Mithuna?" Grissom waited for a nod from Captain Kaplean before keying the destination planet into the nav computer.

"The jump gate personnel are requesting ident." Communications Officer Shimada glanced over her shoulder at the Captain. At his grimace, she turned back to her station,

"Sending anonymous code set. Ident request has been pulled."

"What is our arrival time, Mr. Grissom?" asked Captain Kaplean.

"Arrival to Mithuna will be within 5 days, sir."

The Captain closed his eyes and snorted, "Ms. Shimada, check with the gate personnel for any news from the planet or system. Inform me of anything out of the ordinary."

"Understood, sir."

Captain Kaplean stood up and headed toward the ready room, "The bridge is yours, Lieutenant Hayley."

"Sir, yes sir," responded the Lieutenant.

***

Barney stumped his way out of the back offices of Reverie Station and wiped at his mouth while he cursed. The things you had to do to help those you loved.

The physical acts themselves had been surprisingly simple. "These backwater station rabble have no sense of creativity." Luckily, he had gotten a pretty solid lead in return, but the cost made him feel sick inside.

He grumbled his way down the hallway. Those two Johns in the back office were probably disparaging the virtues or lack thereof for all Titans. Nothing new to him, so what was it about this time that bothered him so much? He stopped and glared into the crowds as they walked by. Maybe the priest was right. Maybe he and his ilk, as she called them, were only meant for one purpose... that kind. He shook himself. "Why am I letting you mess with my head?"

"I am, who I am," he bellowed into the air. "You don't get to choose that for me or tell me otherwise!"

A passerby stopped and backed away from him, "Okay mister, whatever you say. I'm just going to give you some space, alright?"

Barney glared directly at the fellow, "I'm not talking to you. I'm talking to a dead woman."

"Uh, okay?"

"Out of my way." Barney marched past the guy and left him standing there confused.

***

As the M33 settled into orbit around Mithuna, the bridge crew did their best to ignore the raised voices emanating from the ready room.

Captain Kaplean's voice rang harshly as his fist slammed against his desk, "You didn't need to kill all of them! You went too far! May I remind you, this is my command."

Dr. Wyeth's voice barked in disbelief, "Your command? You best know your place, peasant. This is my mission and you follow my orders." An unsettling smile lit upon her lips, "And I went as far as was needed. We have a name and a ship, don't we? Without me here, you'd still be floundering."

He glared at the haughty woman and his hands curled into fists, "Get off my bridge."

Dr. Wyeth stomped through the hatch as Captain Kaplean reentered the bridge. The crew sat a bit straighter as he took his seat. The arguments between the Captain and Dr. Wyeth had been escalating of late. The two had kept their general dislike of one another under wraps. Since their first altercation, their quarrels had only intensified.

"Any news, Ms. Shimada?" asked the Captain.

She pulled the latest update from the planet and perused it quickly. "Nothing major. There was a gunfight in the port. Most of the transgressors have already left the planet. Hmm. Multiple bodies were recently found in a low orbit, though. They have been stored at the morgue for identification."

"How many bodies?" the Captain asked.

She totaled the list, "Thirteen bodies were retrieved, sir. Well... Hmmm... That's odd... "

"What is, Ms. Shimada?"

Her brow wrinkled momentarily, "Two of the bodies were Titans, sir. I didn't know they traveled outside their home system."

Captain Kaplean slid back into his chair. "It's a rare occurrence, Ms. Shimada, but it does happen." He scratched at his lower lip, "Keep an eye on that one. See if you can find anything else that concerns them." His hand dropped to his lap and his fingers tensed. "Lieutenant Hayley, inform Dr. Wyeth that once the lander is prepped, we will be heading to the surface."

"Understood sir."

nine

Heart of Oak

Anton woke abruptly to a splash of cold liquid in his face. Two people held him up by his arms while a third man slapped him across the face. There were laughs as he shrank back from the strike.

The man grabbed him by the shirt and shook him, "Awake yet, cheater?"

Anton blinked until the water no longer blinded him. The guy holding his collar looked strangely familiar. Yes, he recognized him from the gaming table. He glanced to his left and right. There was maybe five or six total. None of them appeared to be packing, so it was just a beat down for bruised egos. He grinned, might as well get it over with then.

"Hey!   It's   the   bunch   of

incompetents!" Anton shook his head, "I've played against some craptastic players before, but you guys take the cake. Well, I mean that's the only way you idiots would get the cake. It sure as hell wouldn't be by skill."

The man holding his collar belted him in the mouth while the two that held his arms pushed in and arched his back. Anton's head rocked back, and he felt his lip split as his blood sprayed through the air.

"Wow. Were you born on a station? It must be hard for you boon-dock boys to get big and strong... what with the lack of decent gravity out here?" Anton rolled his eyes at the two holding his arms, "Am I right? Man hits like a moon-born."

A lady in the back of the alley muffled a laugh as Anton was struck again and his eyebrow tore open. He suffered a couple of blows to the body and he just chuckled while trying to suck in a breath.

Once he was able to catch his breath he spat in the guy's face and blathered, "One more time. With feeling!"

This set the entire group off and they charged in. He went down under a rain of blows and kicks. He did the best he could to protect his face, but the back of his head bounced off the floor. Suddenly he felt one of them being pulled off him. He heard a surprised cry that disappeared into the distance before there was a thud. Another one was thrown off and a small hand pulled him out.

"Barney? That you?" Anton cracked his eyes open and watched the Titan throw those who had been beating on him against the bulkheads of the station.

"Course it is. You think anyone else is going to bother looking for you?" Barney slapped his hands together and yanked him up. "Let's get out of here before the station mercs come down here."

Anton slipped his arm around Barney's shoulder, "How'd you know where to find me?"

Barney smiled at him, "Look for the best place for a beat down. Come on, I've got a lead."

Anton laughed through his bloodied teeth, "Ha, me too."

***

Dr. Wyeth waited until the hatch to her cabin closed. Her hands curled into fists. "Damn that man for getting in my way, again!"

She slid into the chair built into her desk and massaged her temples. How dare he tell her how to handle her mission. Who was he, but a dirty outer-system lowlife? "Given his rank to make the poor feel like they are part of the Consortium. Nothing but fools to be used up and spit out in their time."

A blinking light on her data pad

caught her eye. She pulled it closer and brought up the source of the indicator. A communique from a contact on Mithuna opened up on her screen. It took a moment for her systems to decode the message. As she read it, a smile curled her lips. She quickly wiped the message clear and began typing a reply. Once she was done, she encrypted it and prepped it for sending.

Her comm chimed and Lieutenant Hayley's voice came through, "Doctor? The Captain wanted to inform you that an expedition will be heading to the planet soon."

"Thank you, Lieutenant. Please tell the Captain that I will be joining the expedition."

"Of course..."

Dr. Wyeth interrupted, "Now, set up a tight beam to the planet's surface."

The comm channel was quiet but she felt the ship roll to starboard and settle into a new orbit. Lieutenant Hayley's voice came through the comm, "The ship's trajectory has been changed to allow for a direct comm. The tight beam has been initiated."

Dr. Wyeth found the open channel and shunted her scrambled message into it. A couple minutes later, her data pad chimed with a 'Received' message.

As she destroyed her copy of the message, she said, "Thank you for your assistance, Lieutenant."

***

Captain Kaplean watched with interest as Lieutenant Hayley finished her conversation with the Doctor. As the Lieutenant closed down the tight beam machinery, she glanced at the Captain and gave a small nod.

Communications Officer Mariko stated, "Chief Bull says the lander is prepped for dust-off."

"Let the Chief know I am on the way. Lieutenant Hayley, you're with me."

The Lieutenant nodded and followed the Captain off the bridge. The two officers headed to the closest lift and waited for it to reach their deck. As the door opened, they stepped in and held back for the doors to close.

After the lift began its descent, Captain Kaplean looked over at the Lieutenant, "We should be out of the hearing of the curious. What did the Doctor want?"

"She sent a direct comm to the surface. The message was scrambled and I didn't have a chance to decode it."

"Did you get anything?"

The Lieutenant pulled out her data pad, "Only it's final destination, sir. It's headed to Council Prime on Jard. Directly to the office for the House of Khanda."

The Captain was quiet as he rolled this fact over and over in his mind. The Doctor hadn't been lying about having friends in high places. The House of Khanda was easily the most powerful of the twenty-three ruling families of the Consortium. They hadn't gotten their power quietly and held onto it tightly. Citizens who questioned their policies had a tendency to disappear.

"Thank you, Lieutenant. Please continue monitoring her communications."

The Lieutenant nodded in response and fell into parade rest for the remainder of the trip to the hangar.

***

Derain's feelings sank as he rode the lift down with Detective Mmeli. His old friend had been surprised to see him but had expected him, too. Even though Derain's family was a relatively small bunch, he thought he'd meet up with one or two of them by now. On top of that, Thando had also mentioned something about a funeral.

Maybe his grandfather Mullion had finally passed on. The man was old even by spacer standards and that would fit with the family dealing with sorry business. It could even explain why the house was empty when he had gone to it.

The lift stopped and the doors parted. Detective Mmeli waved him through and led him down the gloomy hallway. Some of the odd green tiles on the wall had fallen to join bits of detritus gathered in the corners and along the edge of the floor. They walked past a few entryways until they reached the battered metal door at the end of the hall. Thando knocked politely before he stepped inside. Derain followed him in.

"Stay here a minute, would you?" asked Inspector Mmeli.

Overall, the lighting in the morgue was dim. There were spotlights set up over individual tables, but most of them were off. Thando went further inside to speak to the coroner. She nodded and rolled a table over to the freezer. A body from the freezer was placed on the table and she slid it over to one of the spotlights in the back. The spotlight clicked on and the beam highlighted the unopened body bag.

Thando then began to gesticulate wildly at the coroner who just shook her head back. From Derain's perspective, the conversation became heated when his friend pointed him out. The coroner indicated another dark corner of the morgue, threw up her hands, then headed for the door.

She tore her gloves off as she passed Derain, "Sorry for your loss."

"Hey Derain, come on over," called out Thando.

Derain shook himself at her comment and went through the door. He joined the detective at the lit-up table. It was a matter of moments as the bag was unzipped and pulled away from the face inside. Even cleaned up, the head was a mess. Ragged skin flaps from the forehead down to the back of the neck had been sewn closed.

Detective Mmeli pointed to the burn mark on the chest over the heart, "As you can see from these bruises, the victim was held down with an electric prod against his chest until his heart stopped or his cybernetic system shut down. We're not really sure. His body is old tech and, uh, we don't do this to people anymore." He glanced at Derain, "Kind of barbaric if you ask me. Anyway, once the victim stopped moving, they proceeded to cut the skin away from the head. A recess was found in the skull for a short cylindrical object, about eighty millimeters in length and thirty millimeters in width. Any idea what it might've been?"

"I think it's a cybernetic memory core," answered Derain. "Don't take that for gospel. That's a guess, at best."

"It's more than we had. I'll just list you as an anonymous source."

Derain brooded for a moment, "Anything else found on his person?"

"Just personal effects. His ship was auctioned off by the space port for unpaid docking fees. He'd been dead a couple weeks before we recovered the body and that was over a month ago." Detective Mmeli gazed at Derain and noticed his seeming preoccupation. "This one personal?"

Derain looked up, "I'm working on a missing person case and she just happens to be a deep spacer. Unfortunately, the leads I've had keep pointing to dead ends. Dead deep spacer ends. This is the second one I've come across with the same M.O. And I've heard stories of a third in the same condition. This case isn't looking good."

Thando pondered while absently scratching at his chin, "Same M.O. huh?"

"Yep. One missing, three dead, and only four others living last I checked. And the news is so slow that the number of living could have dropped lower by now."

Thando put his hand on Derain's shoulder and gave it a light squeeze, "Well I hate to bring you more bad news, but I've got something else to show you before you go."

Detective Mmeli grabbed a spotlight and dragged it over to the dark corner of the morgue. There were multiple tables in this area and each one was burdened with a loaded body bag. He set up the light and proceeded to unzip each bag to expose the faces.

He waited until Derain came over to his side. "You aren't supposed to be viewing this, but I'm doing this because of our friendship. I can write you down for the coroner as identifying the bodies."

Derain's whole face was stricken with horror.

Thando grabbed him by both shoulders, "I need you to get through this as quickly and emotionlessly as possible. The coroner said some scary fellas are looking for you and she went to the Chief Superintendent to cover her ass. So, get this done and get out. I'll tell you all I know while you look."

Derain looked down at the battered face of his father. Someone had beaten him to death. His eyes tracked over to the next table and saw his brother. Further away was his mother, sister, and his aunt. Some of the bags were smaller, tiny in comparison to the adult-sized bags. His eyes hurt from the strain and his throat locked up, but he checked every single bag. His cousins were nestled inside. His nephews and nieces. It was too much to bear.

His eyes burned red and he whispered past the lump that sat in his throat, "My entire family?"

Thando nodded sadly. Derain sank forward and had to catch himself on the table's edge. His body shuddered while his fingers gripped ever tighter onto the metal surface.

The glare he threw at the detective made him shrink back. Derain had had a reputation for being easy to violence. That fire was something Mmeli remembered and did not want to experience. Thando grabbed at Derain's arm, but he jerked away.

"Who did this?"

The detective headed for the door to the morgue, "You need to get out of here. I'll tell you on the way out."

Derain gathered himself and hurried

Jon Gray Lang

after his old friend.

On their way up the stairwell, Thando reiterated everything he knew, "It was a Consortium team. Like no team I had ever seen. Really dark ops. They came in looking for you, but since you weren't here, they grabbed your family. The interrogation was brutal. I... I don't think any of them knew a damn thing."

As they reached the street-side door, Thando stopped him, "I'm really sorry about this. They may still be looking for you, so you should get off-planet soon as you can." He shut the door as soon as Derain cleared it.

Derain stood alone in the alley. The damage was done. No way to save them. Nothing left to do but find the murderers and make them pay. Even if it took him the rest of his life.

***

The Temptation was one hell of a crazy club. The lighting was hazy, and the smells were horrendous, but the place was packed. There were dancers, male, female, and non-binary, in cages suspended from the ceiling. The music was loud, and the crowd was unapologetic. Jacquie really dug the vibe.

As the lady at the desk had said, there were plenty of genorg miners in the place. Maybe it was because she had gotten used to having genorgs all over her ship, but it felt rather comforting to have

Jon Gray Lang

so many around now. The Lieutenant, on the other hand, seemed a bit more nervous than usual.

"What's going on Galena? You seem jumpy."

She shyly smiled back as she glanced up at one of the dancers in the suspended cages. Jacquie just started laughing. She almost spilled her drink from laughing at Galena's discomfort.

"I'd never thought about it, but this is probably a new experience for you." Jacquie chortled.

Galena nodded and took a long swig from her drink, "Why are they gyrating in such a manner?"

Jacquie set her drink down and gazed back at her. "It's for titillation. To get your dander up."

"Dander?" Galena looked on, confused. "Watching them does not give me the urge to fight."

A leer curled the corner of the Captain's lips as she pointed to her crotch. Galena's eyes widened as she stuttered "oh" and turned beet red. Jacquie could no longer contain herself and fell back into the couch, cackling madly. Galena's blush steadily deepened.

"Oh, I'm sorry. I'm sorry. I've just never seen anyone turn that color." Jacquie struggled to keep the giggles under control.

When Galena shrugged away in hurt anger, Jacquie reached out and cupped her shoulder.

She pulled her around and placed her hands over Galena's, "Sometimes I forget that your life experiences are... uneven. You have seen and done things that I can't begin to imagine, but many things that I take for granted you have not done." Her hands fell to her lap, "I didn't mean to embarrass you. Please accept my apology."

The words sounded bitter, but sincere as Galena replied, "It is accepted."

The lights bounced across the walls and the music thumped away during the long, uncomfortable silence between the two of them. Galena gave a sidelong glance to Jacquie. Jacquie grinned wickedly and dragged her to the dance floor. They both relaxed and began giggling as they moved to the pulsing rhythm.

"Hey, you're getting pretty good!" shouted Jacquie over the music.

Galena grabbed the Captain's hand and dipped her quickly before spinning her away. Jacquie clapped with glee as she sauntered back. They began to mirror each other's movements as they swayed back and forth. A circle slowly formed around them, and the room erupted with clapping in time to the beat. When the song ended, the crowd whistled and cheered the dancing duo, who dramatically bowed in mock appreciation. Then Jacquie and Galena made their way back to the couch where they collapsed onto the cushions and convulsed into howling laughter.

"You with that dip and spin!" Jacquie

raved. "I was not expecting that!"

"Glad I can surprise you," Galena chirped. "I learned so much more when I was trying to teach my sisters to dance. It was oddly helpful."

"Luli's a great teacher. By Tom, I miss that woman."

Galena's expression sobered, "I miss her too. We will find her Jacq, we will. I didn't hear any rumors. Did you pick up any leads at the bar?"

At the slow shake of her head, Galena asked, "Have we heard from Anton or Derain?"

"Not a word. Even though it's faster than traveling by ship, communications travel slowly," Jacquie muttered into the song break.

Galena nodded in understanding and gripped her friend's hand tightly. Jacquie squeezed it back. Their hands parted and Galena's slid into her lap.

"Jacq... may I ask you a personal question?"

"Of course! There shouldn't be any secrets between us." Jacquie took a pull on the drink she had raised to her lips.

Galena asked nervously, "Are you recreating with the bounty hunter?"

Jacquie coughed into her glass as she tried to keep from spewing the liquor all over the table. "What gives you that idea?" she sputtered.

Galena indicated the dancers and pointed at her crotch, "The two of you are alone together frequently. You seem to have a special relationship."

Jacquie blinked a few times. "We were friends with benefits a while ago." The Captain frowned at the blank expression on the Lieutenant's face, "We recreated together with no strings attached. It was nothing deeper than having some fun, or, umm... Stress relief."

Jacquie could feel the next question just begging to be asked. She blew out a pent-up breath. "Might as well get it over with," she muttered.

She turned squarely to Galena and leaned back into the couch. "I know you want to know how he got on board the Matilda. I can see it on your face. I'll go you one further and tell you exactly why he wanted to be on the ship, too."

"I am listening."

Jacquie smirked at the deadpan response. "Let's see. Rabbit had left, so it was just me, Lu and Barney." She felt a pang in her heart when she said their names. "We uh, we had a long layover on Fortune's Blunder. Matilda's right engine had gotten something jammed in it and had burned up. Barney needed time to..." there was that pang again. "Barney couldn't get the repair done in orbit, so we were stuck on that rock for most of a week."

Jacquie's eyes sparkled as she recounted, "Luli had lined up a few club shows with another deep spacer to bide the time. And, you know me, being idle just isn't my way. After partying by myself a couple of nights, I was feeling pretty lonely. I still wasn't used to Anton being gone, even though it had been a few months by then."

She stopped for a moment and Galena edged forward on her seat. "It was one of... no, it was the last one of Luli's shows. Barney said..." a small stab hit her heart. "Barney said the repairs were done and the cargo was loaded onto the Matilda. The contract was for a long haul on a tight schedule, so we had to leave on time. Well anyway, I went to the show and I was still feeling lonely. So I had a few drinks and checked out the menu. There was this guy standing alone under one of the spotlights. He was well dressed, had his hair slicked back into a queue, and looked like he really had his shit together. Now, I wasn't looking for more than a one-nighter and he carried himself with an aloofness that just screamed perfection."

As she took a swig, Galena did the same. "I sauntered over and we got to talking. There was a spark between us, a little fire if you know what I mean."

She continued even though Galena shook her head in an emphatic no. "I was pretty loose by then. A handful more drinks and I was downright wanton. I was on the hunt and he was my prey. I stalked him, Galena. I stalked him, trapped him, and after a ride back to the Matilda, I had my way with him. It was everything I needed, and then I passed out."

Galena's face flushed at this

confession and Jacquie just grinned at her. "Luli got us off-planet on time and Barney's repairs held. I woke up late and lo and behold, he was still there... Still in my bunk. I cursed him and I cursed myself and tried to get dressed at the same time." She laughed at the memory, "He must've been very confused. Even more so when he found out we weren't planet side anymore."

Her smile dropped, "But the joke was on me. He had been tracking me the whole time. Seems the Matilda used to belong to his family, and he wanted it back. Having me may have kinked his plans some, but that's the breaks."

She took a long swallow and set her empty glass down. "He still wants the Matilda. We argue about that sometimes, but he hasn't left since that night. I think this is the longest he's been off the ship since I brought him on board."

"Oh. You would not believe the amount of ribbing I got from Lu and Barney once they set eyes on him. Seriously, it was like every day. Meals were crazy for the first few months, but then it became normal. His work and ours synced together well and he fit in with our little bunch."

She felt an ache in her chest as she thought back to the three of them laughing at her expense, enjoying each other's company, and just being together. The sudden urge to hug Barney and Luli hit her hard.

"I miss her, Galena. I really do." Jacquie wiped at the tear that formed in the corners

Jon Gray Lang

of her eyes.

"Look at me getting all maudlin. You want another cocktail?" Jacquie asked as she cracked a wistful smile.

Jacquie acknowledged Galena's affirmative nod and weaved her way back to the bar. Galena, feeling a bit like a fish out of water, looked forward to taking the edge off with the second drink.

Jacquie sidled up to the counter and ordered another round. Glancing around, she noticed the club was leaning more toward the genorg quotient and that change had been pretty sudden.

She shouted to the bartender, "Do the miners have a day off or something?"

He looked over his shoulder and the glass in his hand dropped to the floor, "Oh my..."

Gunfire erupted in the background and Jacquie hit the deck. She tried to spot Galena while also keeping an eye out for danger, but everything was a blur. People screamed and ran in all directions. It was a madhouse. Fragments of plastic and metal spun through the air as an explosion tore the end of the bar apart.

Jacquie crawled across the floor to where she had left the Lieutenant. It was hard going, and she got stepped on, but she finally made her way to Galena's side. They sheltered behind one of the couches that were clustered throughout the club. With a simultaneous nod, they pulled out their pistols.

Jon Gray Lang

One of the dance cages plummeted and cracked open like an egg spilling its dancer out onto the liquor-soaked carpet. A genorg clutching a rifle riddled the ceiling with bullets. She was immediately flanked by two more and a few genorgs guarded the exit. Slowly the Temptation quieted down. In the sudden silence, you could just faintly hear gunfire and explosions mixed with screams echoing from down the hallway.

A genorg moved to the center of the dance stage and surveyed the crowd, "If everyone keeps quiet, no one will get hurt. Is this understood?"

Not a peep came from the people trapped in the club. In a sudden burst of movement, a man ran for the doorway, but he skittered across the room as he was shot repeatedly from behind. His dead body came to rest right next to the Captain and the Lieutenant. They both looked down in astonishment and then back up to the stage.

Jacquie rasped, "What the hell is going on?"

Galena raised a finger to her lips and leaned into the back of the couch. Jacquie nodded and kept an eye on the other side of the room. She watched as a drone ran into the club, whispered into the ear of the one on the stage, then headed back out into the hall.

The genorg spoke to the room, "We do not wish any further bloodshed. Please throw down your weapons." All of the genorgs leveled their rifles over the room. "We have liberated this station and the mine below in the name of the First Soldier! All hail Lieutenant Chadov!"

The room rang with shouts of "Hail! Hail! Hail!"

Jacquie stared at Galena in complete confusion. Galena shrugged in response. Together, they threw their pistols to the ground and raised their hands in surrender.

ten

Freight Train

Luli gazed blankly out of the port window and truly felt the emptiness of space. Her captors had given her free rein of the room once they had finished breaking her fingers. With nothing to splint them with, she had done the best she could to get them reseated into their joints properly. But they were still useless and they hurt like hell.

She remembered passing out at least twice from the pain and her systems informed her she was running a slight fever now. She smiled, "Even so, I feel pretty lucid at the moment."

A sudden movement out in space beyond the window caught her eye. As she tried to find it again, she absently tapped a finger against the bulkhead. She sucked in a breath and squeezed her eyes shut from the resulting burst of pain.

Jon Gray Lang

It took a moment, but she regained control of her breathing. Her eyes opened and she looked out the window once more. The woozy feeling was affecting her ability to track the movement she had seen. Her vision blurred and her eyes blinked closed. She forced them open and searched for the object again. She finally found it against the darkness. It was a person in a spacesuit, but there was something strange about it. The faceplate glowed from the inside and it was moving toward her. The light from it grew brighter until she was blinded.

Forgotten memories hit her and she whispered in awe, "I remember you."

***

Anton floated through the empty station bay toward slot 2491. Barney had discovered that this ship was pulling more oxygen than its crew of three should warrant. Barney had staked out the entry port while Anton mended, and the crew always left in groups of two. But they always returned with enough food to feed two more. That remained the case until earlier today.

Anton now could recognize the three of them from just about anywhere. They carried themselves like brawlers and street toughs, but they stayed out of trouble. "Maybe they found God," joked Barney.

While Anton tailed them, Barney had

gotten the schematics of the ship. The Demetrius was an odd boat. Part of her was an original Sol system build stripped from one of the old colony ships. Another part was more of a recent addition, only from the last decade or so. She looked like she had been cobbled together from a pile of wreckage. From what the records showed, she was.

Anton straightened up, turned on his magnetic boots, and clicked to the ship's hull. Up close, she looked even worse. Ugly welds dotted the hull and poorly seated rivets stuck up from the surface. He searched for the communication array but couldn't find it.

"Where is this thing again, Barney?" he asked.

There was a long pause before Barney responded, "What do you see right now?"

"Just a bunch of nothin'."

Anton could feel Barney tweaking the bridge of his nose through the comm, "Rabbit? You know I need more than that. So, again, what do you see?"

Anton looked along the hull, "Looks like I landed near the engines. At a guess, about halfway between the two cones."

"Thank you for playing along. Head forward. There should be a dip, possibly a break, about midway up. Once there, let me know what you see again. Cyclops out."

Anton worked his way forward. Barney was becoming increasingly touchy of late.

Jon Gray Lang

Not that he didn't have good reason since he had practically raised Jacq. It made Anton angry just thinking about how she had tossed Barney aside as if all their time together had meant nothing. Family was important. Family was everything. How could she do that to him?   More importantly, what would she do to him if she ever found out he had been crew on that pirate ship?

He kept moving along when his right boot hit empty space and he tipped forward. His boot clicked to the flip side of the slab of hull he was on. He popped the left boot, did a full rotation and was inside the break. To be honest, it was more like a separate piece of the ship. In fact, it was a chunk from a completely different one.

***

Barney flipped the comm switch as Anton's voice came through, "I'm at the break as you called it. Looks like someone harvested an old station compartment and welded it on. How does this thing not just fly apart?"

Barney muttered, "Good welds? How would I know? You're the one out there."

"It was more of a rhetorical question," Anton chirped back. "Anyways, what am I supposed to be looking for out here?"

Barney scrolled through the schematics until he found the communications cluster. He enlarged the image and zoomed in. "It should look like a tightly packed set of antennas. It might be on the other half though. Keep an eye out."

"Aye, aye acting Captain. Anton out."

Barney rolled his eyes. He went back to the schematic of the ship and stared at it. Besides being ugly, there was something off about it. For one thing, it was an awfully large craft for a crew of three. For another, it wasn't outfitted as a shipping trawler. If it was just for personal use, it was a brute about it.

He scrolled through the ship's principal dimensions and his eyes rested on a set of numbers. That thing had a ton of mass. What was on her that required that much mass? The engine set up didn't look like it needed something that heavy. It set the gears in his engineering mind to work. His focus broke when the comm kicked on.

"Think I've got it. I'm wiring in the tap now."

It only took a few minutes before Anton added, "All done. On my way back."

"Hurry it up. We don't know when they plan on leaving."

"Double timing it. Anton out."

Barney ran through the comm channels until he found the frequency for the tap. It was quiet, but the signal came through strong and clear. When the Demetrius went through a gate, they'd get the bead on its destination. They would follow them through and leave messages behind for the Matilda and the Waratah. Since they were the only ship to have a lead on them, they didn't have a choice except to keep on its tail.

***

His coming was seen as a sign of the end and the old spacer chant came easily to Luli's lips, "Death and danger. Here comes the Major. Death and danger. Here comes the Major. Death and danger..."

He had only been a man in the grand scheme of things. Sinner to some and saint to others. His life story was simple, but in the great beyond he was both protector and curse. She was taken back to when she had been little. If she focused on the light, she could hear her long-dead preacher's voice as she spoke of the patron saint for spacers.

"He came, some say, in a flash of light, others, in a burst of flame. He came in the night, from the darkness that surrounds. He came from nowhere and has become all things. He is here among us or out there in the darkness, the darkness that surrounds. For he is that which lights the way."

"May the Major hold the tiller. May the Major guide the ship."

"He shelters those of us in times of need and his darkness grants us safe passage. His light burns the way for those he has come to collect. Be it for wrong or right, his ship needs a crew and he will come to collect."

"May the Major hold the tiller. May the Major guide the ship."

Her father had told her stories of Major Tom that shed some of the mystique from the preacher's prayers. He had only been a man when the humans of Old Earth were just breaching the confines of their home planet. It was in the very dawn of space travel and he had been sent up alone. His capsule had been damaged, and he ejected from it, only to burn up on the edge of the Earth's atmosphere.

Songs were sung about him. Within those songs spoke the loss of innocence for humanity in its exploration of space. But he was still just a man, a legend maybe, but still a man. As humanity built their space stations and colonized the ancient solar system, people began to speak of seeing the man in a spacesuit with a brightly lit faceplate. Then those people died or disappeared. And the man who was a legend was believed to be a God.

Or a devil. The two beliefs intermixed, and he became both. He would be called upon by some when disaster was imminent and he was cursed by others for the same reason. And the stories of his sightings grew. Luli was sure that there were other colonies of humans who still called upon him just as she was sure there were humans out there who reviled his name. The Major knew and saw all.

Jon Gray Lang

She turned back to the window and the spaceman was pressed against the plas-glass of the window. Her face reflected in the glow. She could barely make out the long-forgotten flag on his sleeve and scratched lettering on his suit through the glare.

The faceplate cleared and she could see her father smiling back at her. Suddenly she felt his arms encircle her like he had done when she was little. She looked up into his face and he held her close.

"Sing for me, my child. Sing for me my little Luli Qing..."

Her face broke out into a happy grin, "I'll sing for you daddy, I'll sing for you."

Her voice broke the silence in the room as she sang softly, "Freight train, freight train, run so fast, please don't tell what train I'm on..."

eleven

Go Get the Ax

The jump gate for the Junction system spiraled open and the Independence slid through. A sigh escaped Commander Keri as she keyed in the fake ident and sent it to the gate personnel. Silence ruled the bridge until they were granted permission to continue. They had made it through another gate under their false ident.

Mr. Leon stood on the bridge with Delta as Rosa brought the ship into its port. Once Rosa received confirmation that the airlock was latched to the station, she began to power down the vessel for their stay.

"Captain Delta? The ship is yours," Rosa gave a small bow and stepped back.

Delta rankled at the giving of rank, but Mr. Leon touched her lightly on the arm and gave a slight nod. She completed the ritual that they had performed at a handful of stations now, "Thank you, Commander. You may go about your business."

Rosa inclined her head again as Delta turned and stepped through the hatch of the bridge. Her shoulders slumped just a little bit before she adjusted their posture. She glanced over at Mr. Leon who stood by and appraised her. Mr. Leon had been acting a little differently since they had met up with the Copperhead. Her head tilted as she stared quizzically back at him. A tiny smile appeared on his face as he stepped forward and entwined his arm in hers.

"How is being in my employment working out for you, Ms. Keri?"

She sized him up for a moment before she answered, "It's better than death. To be honest, it's better than my last gig. I don't like what we're doing with these soldiers, but as an indentured servant, it's not my place to complain." She was quiet for a long while before she asked, "How am I working out as your newest employee, Mr. Leon?"

"Oh, I am quite pleased with you, Ms. Keri. Quite pleased, indeed." He confided to her slowly, "Don't worry about the genorgs; they'll warm to you soon enough. It's included in their training and indoctrination."

She continued to let him lead her down to the cargo bay but kept quiet for the rest of the journey. As they entered the cargo bay, she watched as Delta and Gamma divided their platoons into squads of ten. It bothered her that many of the genorgs would not be continuing their journey aboard the Independence. They would be assigned to other ships as cargo and flitted off to various points of the Consortium as unpaid workers. But what could she do when the genorgs themselves didn't seem to have a problem with it?

She felt a bit melancholy that the genorgs treated her as an outsider. At the same time, that personal distance did make it easier for her to watch them disappear into the void, most likely never to be heard from again. She still pondered what Mr. Leon had said to them to make them agree to this choice, this life. He had consistently proven that he was quite the silver-tongued devil and the genorgs themselves were pretty naive in general. But still, she wondered what exactly had passed between them.

Mr. Leon pulled at her arm to bring her to a halt as the small teams of genorgs headed off to the ships that would take them to their new work camps. She noticed that Gamma was getting ready to leave with the last group. She stepped forward, pressed her hand into Gamma's, and shook it vigorously.

"I wish you well on your journeys, Gamma."

Gamma stopped and looked down at Rosa's hand in hers. She grasped it firmly and repeated the words back to her, "I wish you well on your journeys, Rosa." She let go of her hand and followed after the other genorgs.

Rosa stared down at her hand then slowly let it fall to her side as she watched Gamma leave. She gazed over the cargo bay and did a quick count. Around fifty of the genorgs would be staying on board with Delta in charge. The other three hundred and thirty odd had been left at various planets and stations all to be shipped off to other sites. A wave of depression hit her.

"How did I come to this?" she lamented.

Mr. Leon strode up behind her, "Oh, I think you are quite aware of the decisions you made to end up here. But, if you keep on living, is it not true that you still have a chance? A chance for peace of mind, a chance for happiness, yes?" He took her by the arm, "Please come with me."

Rosa shook off his grip and headed toward the airlock. Mr. Leon shrugged and followed her out. Rosa stopped at the end of the companionway and waited for him to take the lead into the station. He headed off to the right and she sped up to walk beside him.

Mr. Leon looked over at her, "This is a simple check-in, but I may need your assistance. Have you ever acted as a bodyguard, Ms. Keri?"

She smirked in reply.

"Oh yes. Of course, Mr. Melende."

He let that last statement hang in the air as they joined up with the larger crowds on the station known as the Silk Road. Rosa looked around in amazement at the sheer variety of goods that were here.

"Impressive isn't it?" Mr. Leon stated. "I can still remember the first time I came to this station. I had never seen anything like it. I was quite young, and I hadn't been exposed to much of anything except the inside of the hospital where I was raised."

A strange half-smile crossed his lips, "But due to some personal failings, the doctors had come to the decision that I should experience more. Dr. Saric had initially been quite against it. But I wasn't improving in the manner that they had hoped. So, they brought me here to see what I would learn and to monitor how I reacted."

He noticed that Rosa was listening intently. "As you can probably guess, I thought this place was magical. I had never seen such a variety and number of the citizenry in one place before. I couldn't even grasp the idea that there were more people in our little corner of the universe. My doctors found it quite amusing. But this place opened my eyes to the simple idea that there is more out there than I could possibly imagine. And if there is more out there than I could imagine, then there must be more out there than Dr. Wyeth or Dr. Saric could, too. Seeing this wonderful place was the first step in my desire to see more."

He turned to her, "Do you know the history of this station?"

"Not really, to be honest."

Jon Gray Lang

His cheeks colored from the large grin on his face, "Well, I wanted to know more about this place. The doctors finally relented and gave me access to the histories of the Consortium. As I'm sure you know; jump gates are constructed within a certain distance of each other, but mostly in habitable or resource-heavy systems. But there is nothing here except dead space, you say! And you would be right. This little jump gate functioned as sort of an in-between for many systems that were only a jump away." His arms opened to encompass everything, "The tiny station meant to be temporary housing for the builders of the jump gate began to be used as a local commerce point for the closest systems. Rumors about the station went out and other traders and merchants began to arrive in droves. The little station grew until it became a major trade hub and the wares that were bought and sold quickly grew in response. The station was humorously nicknamed the Silk Road and it became an attraction; a city of wonders as well as a place famous for its illicit dealings. As time passed, there was very little that couldn't be purchased at the Silk Road."

A shy smile flitted across his face and disappeared like a ghost. "I worked hard with the belief that I would get to see more of this grand station, but I was mistaken. My doctors had other plans for me."

Rosa watched as his hands settled to his sides. He came to a stop and closed his eyes. He breathed in deeply and a shudder passed through him as he turned to the left and continued on his way. She hurried to keep up with him. She had thought he was a strange man, but what was this talk of doctors and hospitals?

He reached out a hand and touched her sleeve. She let him do so and he took her hand in his. "Oh, Dr. Wyeth appreciated my drive in doing better, but I was to eventually learn that I would never be released. Do you know what it is to be trapped and know it? To see no way out? As you can imagine, once I realized that there was no way out for me, my drive to succeed failed. I fell far behind their schedule and they became desperate. Apparently, the project that I was a key part of was quite expensive. They worked with their investors and pulled out all the stops. Various experimental treatments were tried. Drug cocktails that sent me to the depths of depression and the heights of mania were poured into me. But it was then that I realized, through failure lay my path to freedom."

"Failure?" Rosa asked confused. "How can failure get you to freedom?"

Mr. Leon grinned at her confusion, "It's quite simple, really. And the best part is that neither of my caretakers figured it out. If I continued to fail, the project would be canceled, and I would no longer be needed. No longer as naive as I once was, I saw no reason to believe that they would ever let me go. Unbeknownst to them, I had learned more than they had meant me to. And lastly,

I had compiled resources that they did not know existed, nor could they possibly imagine."

He brought them to a stop in front of the office district of the station. "With my renewed drive to fail, the project ground to a halt. The funding was pulled shortly afterward. The doctors had to abandon their research and the test subjects, like me, were quietly disposed of. Well, not all of the test subjects."

A cold fury emanated from him, controlled, but ominous. His hands curled into fists. His nails cut into his palms and droplets of blood splashed against the decking. "It cost me more than any single person can ever imagine. I was able to escape. And I escaped to the only place I had ever been. There I used everything I had learned. I made my connections and built my empire. And now we are here."

He smiled at Rosa, "Please take your position here and prevent anyone from entering. I will be back in an hour."

twelve

Company Town

The trip to the morgue on Mithuna had been a tension-filled ride through silence. Dr. Wyeth had forced her way on this trip and neither she nor the Captain spoke more than three words to each other. Mortuary Affairs Officer Cutler had also joined them as the facial recognition records of the Consortium far surpassed those of these planet-bound mercenaries parading as police.

"Captain Kaplean? Sir?" Shimada Mariko's voice came over his personal comm.

He turned to face away from the Doctor, "I am here. What is it, Officer Shimada?"

"I just received a communique from the surface. More bodies have been located and recovered within the system. Identification has already been given and it's a locally-known pirate crew commanded by a Philani Flavio."

"Flavio? What kind of a name is that?" grumbled the Captain.

Dr. Wyeth looked over at Captain Kaplean once she heard the name.

"I am assuming he had a ship. Is there wreckage?" asked the Captain.

Ms. Shimada replied, "He was known to command a vessel named the Garuda. No wreckage was found near the bodies, sir."

"Track anything you can find out about that ship. It might be useful. Captain out." He clicked the comm off and noticed Dr. Wyeth staring at him.

The Captain twisted up his face and relented, "The bodies of a pirate crew known to haunt these travel ways were found orbiting this planet."

It troubled him that the Doctor perked up at this and became much more animated for the remainder of the journey. The runner came to a stop out front of the morgue and the Captain stepped out. Officer Cutler followed him. He handled all the necessary paperwork which allowed the Doctor and the Captain to enter the building quickly.

It was a short jaunt to the elevator and down four floors to the basement. They were ushered into the freezer room where thirteen bodies had been laid out for their inspection. Officer Cutler spoke with the morticians briefly before they hurriedly left the room.

"The room is ours, Captain," he said into the stillness. "Ten of the bodies have been identified as local thugs and miscreants. The two Titans are still unidentified and there is one headless body as well."

"See if you can identify that one first, Mr. Cutler."

"Of course, Captain," he replied.

Officer Cutler stepped over to one of the tables and ran scans on the DNA of the individual as well as the fingerprints. His face lit up and he strode triumphantly over to his Captain.

"We have a hit, sir. This man is none other than Sam Melende, late of the Vogelgesang."

Dr. Wyeth positively crowed in delight at this news, "She was here Captain. She was here!" She danced a jig in the confined space. "We're running out of culprits, Kaplean. She must be hunting them down and now, there are only two more left!"

"The last intel we received stated that she was traveling with the revolutionary Anton Roane. I doubt she is hunting the man," exclaimed the Captain.

But the Doctor ignored him and continued her little dance, "She must have executed that pirate crew before she moved onto these paltry excuses of humans." She stopped moving and turned to Captain Kaplean, "You have regained some of my respect, Captain. Let us hope that this upward trend of yours continues."

'This disturbing woman is chasing after her even more disturbing creature. Like Dr. Frankenstein and his monster in the old fables. And I am helping her. I am her Captain Walton.' The skin of his back rippled downward.

***

By the time that Captain Kaplean had made it back to the M33, Communications Officer Shimada had retrieved some data from the jump gate communication's department. She stood waiting for him at the airlock of the hangar bay.

The prim young woman caught Captain Kaplean's eye as he boarded his ship, "Ms. Shimada? What can I do for you?"

She saluted before she addressed him, "Sir, I have tracked down a few leads from the information I was able to gather from the jump gate travel records."

"Oh? Excellent," he replied as he observed Dr. Wyeth leave the lander. "Please walk with me and tell me on the way."

She skipped a little to catch up, "Of course, Captain." She reviewed her list as they shuffled through the crowd of crew and headed toward the lift. "In regard to the two Titans in the morgue, the jump gate registry did have records of a Titan ship requesting access to Mithuna. The planet's tower listed a Titan ship under the name

Cyclops as having landed a few weeks prior with a crew of two. Strangely, there is no record of it departing the planet, but the jump gate does have it registered as having left a fortnight ago. Also, with a crew of only two aboard."

Captain Kaplean hit the lift button and the doors parted immediately. He stepped inside and was quickly followed by his Communications Officer.

"A documented arrival on planet, but none for a departure? And now we have two Titan corpses, but a crew of two still left the system? Hmm." He turned to Ms. Shimada, "Did the gate registry have a destination for the Cyclops?"

"Um, yes sir. Here it is." She flipped through the records list, "It requested travel to the Prima-Sotra system."

Captain Kaplean mulled that over. There was nothing intrinsically odd about it. Sometimes smaller ships would piggyback on the bigger ones to save on launch fuel usage. It niggled at him. But it wasn't what he was searching for. "Thank you, Ms. Shimada. Was there anything more?"

"Yes sir, there is. The Waratah, the ship that we tracked to this system from Aketi, requested travel to the Aken system. It seems that we just missed her."

"How many were listed on board?"

"Just one," she answered. "I've already sent out a request to the local Aketi system branch to capture his ship."

Captain Kaplean smiled in satisfaction, "That is excellent news. Good work, Ms. Shimada."

The lift doors parted, and he stepped out into the hallway on his way to the bridge. His Communications Officer followed him.

"Sir? I... I have also discovered an anomaly."

He stopped and gave her a quizzical look, "An anomaly?"

She appeared somewhat perturbed as she responded, "Yes Captain. It's about the Garuda."

"Well? What about it?"

"The Captain of the Matilda, one Jacquotte Delahaye, is the one who claimed the salvage on the Garuda. But then it gets a little strange. She handed over ownership to one Galena Chadov." Officer Shimada watched the Captain's face, "Isn't that the genorg we're searching for?"

He glanced down the hallway in both directions. He cupped her elbow and whispered into her ear, "Come with me."

She nodded and followed him onto the bridge and into his ready room. He closed the door behind her and sat behind his desk. He indicated one of the chairs in front of his desk.

He interlaced his fingers as he watched her. "We'll start with this ship, the Matilda okay, Mariko?"

She felt a little strange as the Captain rarely used first names, "Of... of course, Captain." She looked down at her data pad and scrolled through the gate registry. "The Matilda left the system a couple of weeks ago."

"And this Captain Delahaye?"

Mariko shifted over to Identity Files on her data pad. "Jacquotte Delahaye, owner of the merchant ship Matilda. No records beyond her work as a merchant vessel. No planet of origin either. Aah... here is the reason why. Her parents owned the ship before she did."

"Probably born on the freighter, then," Captain Kaplean muttered. "Anything on the parents?"

"They are both listed as victims of a pirate attack. Ownership of the vessel transferred to Captain Delahaye on their death," she replied.

"Any logs of the ship's destination?"

Mariko switched back to the jump gate registry, "It requested permission for travel to system DV2665."

The Captain thoughtfully considered the information. Technically, nothing was out of place. Merchant ships were attacked by pirates and marauders all the time. The cost of having a patrol ship ride-along was cost-prohibitive to many of the independent trawlers. So, many of them had taken to arming themselves for defense. Some merchant ships had even resorted to stalking pirate ships for the salvage.

He forced himself back to the matter at hand. "This Captain Delahaye then handed the salvage rights over to Galena Chadov?"

"Correct, sir."

He exhaled noisily as he pressed his fingers to his temples, "What do we have on the Garuda?"

Mariko scrolled back to the planet Mithuna's records, "After the salvage was approved, the Garuda's name was changed to the Independence. It is captained and owned by one Lieutenant Galena Chadov."

Captain Kaplean wrinkled his brow in consternation, "We're searching the whole of Consortium space for this genorg and now it owns a merchant class ship?" It boggled his mind. "Did the Garuda... the Independence I mean, take on a shipment, or did it leave with an empty hold?"

"Bear with me a moment," Mariko replied. She logged into the Loader's Union records and there was a shipment listed to the Independence. A little more research and she let out a small sigh of satisfaction. "She is listed as shipping goods for Unifreight, Inc. The president is a Mr. Leon."

"First name?" the captain asked.

Mariko's brow wrinkled, "There isn't one on file? That's strange."

Perhaps this Galena Chadov used to travel on the Matilda, perhaps not. It seemed that she now had a ship under her name and she was taking on cargo. Captain Kaplean clapped his hands together. Progress, finally some progress. "Schedule a meeting with this Mr. Leon."

"Of course, Captain."

thirteen

Shadowman

Derain stopped in front of a tall, ordinary office building in downtown Aketi. It had taken some time, but gradually, little hints grew into rumors that produced a solid lead which brought him here. His hope was that the owner of this nondescript structure would help him locate the people responsible for disposing of his kinsman like so much trash.

He cast a long glance down the street to see if anyone was watching, but the way ahead looked clear. He approached the building and stepped through the entrance into a tastefully appointed lobby that revealed no clue as to the owner's true nature. A busy, young and smartly dressed woman stood behind the reception counter and gave him a smile. But a pair of obvious security guards stationed beside the front doors behind Derain made him nervous. So did the immense number of security cameras scattered throughout the lobby. Because of the shady reputation of the building's owner, Derain could readily imagine just how many more hidden cameras and guns were trained on him at this point, as well. The knowledge was unnerving.

As Derain ventured across the lobby, the female attendant approached to stop him, "Mr. Tiwi? The proprietor will see you now. If you would follow me?"

He shrugged and trailed after her. He didn't relish this encounter, but the man had a vast list of connections and Derain knew he might be the only person on this planet who could help. The important question, though, was just what might that 'help' cost? It didn't really matter as there was very little he wouldn't be willing to give in exchange.

The young woman entered a lift and politely held the door open for him. Derain stepped in after her. She keyed a code into a brass panel, then stood at attention beside it. The lift rose with a slight jerk. It eventually settled a few floors up, but Derain wasn't entirely sure just how many. Considering the renowned paranoia of the man who owned this building, the lift actually may have gone down, or it may not have moved at all.

The attendant opened the door and directed Derain to the right and down the hallway. The increased number of armed security visible on this floor was impressive... and intimidating. She led him to a black door and knocked politely. At the invitation, the office door opened and she waved him in. Derain stepped into the room and heard the door click closed behind him.

"Good afternoon, Mr. Tiwi," said a voice from the shadows behind a massive desk. "I hope your travels find you well."

"Well enough, Mr. Leon," Derain replied as he approached the desk.

Mr. Leon smiled in a self-deprecating manner, "Please take a seat." He waited until Derain had settled himself into one of the plush chairs, then asked, "Now... What can I, as a humble businessman, do for you?"

***

Captain Kaplean had his people go through channels generally not used by the Consortium. In his opinion, organized crime as some put it, shouldn't be treated as a known entity by the governing system. But that self-same governing system required an entity such as organized crime when even the Black Ops Division might be under too much scrutiny.

As a result, he found himself here in this office, with his Gunnery Sergeant, Mr. Manny Alvarez. He gazed at the slight man who sat across from him. Mr. Leon's pale green eyes seemed to bore into his soul. The Captain looked away and checked on the Sergeant. He stood in a relaxed stance and took in the entire room. It gave him peace of mind, so he turned back to the strange man.

"Uh, Mr. Leon is it?" At the slight nod, he continued, "Mr. Leon, I require some information and I have come to understand you are a broker for such things."

"Are you listening to rumor and hearsay, Captain Kaplean? Such shocking behavior for an upstanding member of our glorious Consortium. But trying times do call for trying actions, do they not? Even for one of the vaunted shadow teams of our wonderful governing body, yes?" Mr. Leon waited a moment to let that knowledge sink in.

The Captain visibly paled, but he continued, "I have come to understand that a rogue group from an unknown government division may have destroyed your operation in the Spur system. As a representative of the Consortium, I do apologize for the error."

Mr. Leon's face took on the visage of a grin, but there was no humor or forgiveness in it. "Apology accepted Captain. Now, what can my humble shipping company do for you?"

***

Derain's lips curled into a grimace, "Humble businessman, my ass." He leaned forward,

"I need two things, Mr. Leon and I am hoping you can find it in your heart to help me."

Mr. Leon's eyes lit up. "Your requests are personal then? My, my Mr. Tiwi! Personal requests carry a very high price."

"I am aware." Derain sat back and stared into Mr. Leon's strangely unsettling green eyes, "My first request has to do with the murdered deep spacers. In particular, one Bartolo Tufaro."

"Yes. I had heard of his relatively recent passing. It is a sad day when even someone who is considered a celebrity can be discovered dead in a dumpster. It is not a shining moment for our little world, is it, Mr. Tiwi."

"No. It isn't."

Mr. Leon put his finger to his chin as he stared up toward the ceiling, "I may have heard of a ship that left quite soon after the apparent time of death of Mr. Tufaro. Would this be in relation to the disappearance of one Luli Qing? I understand she was snatched away in the middle of the night on Mithuna." A calculating grin lit his face, "How valuable is this information to you?"

"Very."

Mr. Leon set his hands down on his desk. "I have also heard a rumor about the sudden loss of an entire family. Four generations, if the rumors are correct. Strangely, they had the same surname as you carry, Mr. Tiwi. Would you also be looking for information on this very tragic event?"

Derain's face tightened as he softly

snarled, "Yes."

Mr. Leon steepled his fingers and brought them to his lips, "To be perfectly honest, Mr. Tiwi, I could never understand what you must be going through. How hard it must be for you to ask for help from someone like me. Now, of course, we've had dealings in the past, but to be in debt to someone with my type of connections must irk you. Somewhere, deep inside, you must be writhing at the very idea of this meeting."

"Yes."

"But I know things about you too, Mr. Tiwi. I know that you have committed murder before, both in passion and in coldness. For personal reasons and simply for pay. And these are things I appreciate about you, Mr. Tiwi. It is because of these qualities that I feel we can discuss a price that would be amenable to both of us."

"What is it going to cost me?"

***

Captain Kaplean sat back and stared at the little man. '*I could squash you like a bug,*' came to his mind, but he held his tongue. Something about the man irritated him. He felt as if he were being watched, not just by this individual, but many others. Considering who he represented, there must be closed-circuit cameras dotting the entire office. Without knowing where the video of this meeting was being saved or broadcast, it was best to play this clean.

"What can your shipping company do for me?" the Captain asked. "It's pretty straightforward. I just need to know about a delivery that a particular vessel made for your company."

"A shipping manifest? But of course." Mr. Leon clicked on the comm, "Ms. Kwan? Please come to my office with the latest shipping manifests."

The two men waited in relative silence until Kwan Sang arrived. She stepped over to Mr. Leon's desk and pulled up the most recent shipping history. As she brought up the report, she noticed that the Captain was intently watching her employer, who seemed preoccupied with the items on his desk. She suddenly remembered the grisly prize Mr. Leon had stored in the office. *'Or inside his desk,'* she thought. She pulled her thoughts away from that and turned to face the Captain, "What cargo or destination are you looking for?"

"It's more about the ship than the cargo." He studied her to see how she reacted, "The ship I am tracking is known as the Independence. It was a recent acquisition of one Galena Chadov."

She visibly quailed for a moment, but then she resumed the search through her system. It took only a moment or two, but in that time, Captain Kaplean realized she obviously knew something about the vessel or its crew that frightened her. Meanwhile, Mr. Leon blithely looked on without any great concern at all. The man was a conundrum.

Ms. Kwan spoke up, "We contracted the Independence out to deliver a shipment of medical supplies." Before he had a chance to ask why, she continued, "There was a viral outbreak on the moon Nowhere in the Hazard system. Oh! But this manifest shows the supplies are already delivered."

"Do you know where it was scheduled to go to next?"

His hands knotted at her firmly negative head shake. "What about the Matilda, captained by one Jacquotte Delahaye?"

"Here it is," she answered. "We had it sent out to the Toros Colony in the DV2665 system. According to the manifest, it was for mining equipment."

"Mining equipment?" the Captain asked, slightly taken aback.

Sang smiled, "Oh yes. It may not have much to offer as a home, but Toros is a mineral-rich world. The profits to be made there are quite substantial."

"Did you have this ship scheduled for another drop?"

"Hmm, no this was the only shipping destination under our manifest." She answered matter of factly, "Both of these trawlers are independently owned and run. As much as we would like to expand our shipping rights, it does become overly expensive to maintain such a large fleet. We round out our deliveries through the use of contracted independents. Were there any other shipments you had an interest in, Captain?"

"Uh, no. No thank you, Ms. Kwan."

"Is there anything else you require of me, Mr. Leon?" At the slight shake of his head and the tiniest of smiles, she turned to face the two men, "I bid you good day, Captain." At the tiny nod of approval from her employer, she left the room. She had done well.

***

"The price itself is quite small. However, achieving it might be very expensive, Mr. Tiwi," Mr. Leon teased.

"I'll pay it. I'll do whatever needs doing," answered Derain.

"Excellent! I do believe that we can strike a bargain then," Mr. Leon gleefully replied. "Now let's see, the ship that left in such a hurry from our humble little world is a bit of a strange one. She is called the Demetrius if I'm not mistaken."

"Demetrius? Isn't that the name of one of the old colony ships?" Derain quizzed.

Mr. Leon replied, "You know your history. Yes, I do believe it is. She is quite an ugly vessel, if the gossip from the spaceport is true. A cobbled mess of a boat, from all accounts. I have a three-dimensional mock-up of her. Would you care to see it?"

At the nod, Mr. Leon brought it up on his desk holo. He spun the image and rotated it on its axis. "Some of her lines do bear a passing resemblance to an old colony ship, if you look deep enough."

Derain stared at the ship and committed it to memory. She really was a mess. Some idiot had welded canisters and living quarters to the original framework. The thing would never survive a planetfall. "I'm surprised it actually works. From the looks of it, the boat should just fall apart."

Mr. Leon smiled, "I quite agree. It is registered to a conglomerate that in reality is just a shell company for a private investor. I have not worked that out yet. The investor prefers to avoid the limelight, if you get my meaning."

"I think I do," Derain replied.

"Well, anyway, it listed its next port of call as Reverie Station in the Prima-Sotra system. Are you familiar with this system, Mr. Tiwi?" Mr. Leon asked.

"Prima-Sotra?" Derain's mind raced with thoughts of Anton's search for Yannick Specht. "Yes, I believe I've been out that way after a skip at one point."

"Excellent!" cried Mr. Leon. "Then it should be quick work for you, yes?"

Derain wrinkled his brow as he watched the man. Why his sudden interest in this case? What did he have invested in this, if anything?

Jon Gray Lang

There were always more questions than answers with Mr. Leon. Always.

"That is the hope," Derain replied. "Now to my next question."

An odd glow came to Mr. Leon's face as he smiled wryly, "Oh, yes. The one that is ever more personal. One could say it cuts to the core." He tapped at his desk terminal and brought up a three-dimensional mock-up of another ship... and relished the shocked expression that appeared on his guest's face.

"I've seen a ship, no, two ships that have that same configuration," Derain's exclamation shattered the silence.

"Have you? How strange," Mr. Leon purred.

Derain turned and demanded, "Tell me what you know about this vessel. Where did it come from? Whose is it and what are its capabilities?"

"I believe you know its capabilities, Mr. Tiwi," replied Mr. Leon. "As to where it's built, that I do not currently know. As to its owners, that would be the Consortium."

"The Consortium? But why would they go after them?" Derain stood up and gripped the edge of the desk, "What would make a person slaughter my family? Even the children?"

Mr. Leon watched as the gears turned in Derain's head.

Derain muttered in anger, "They've

been after us the entire time. I thought that Sam Melende would be the end of it, but apparently, he was just someone else's lackey."

He began pacing back and forth, "I slipped up somewhere. And they tracked me to my kindred. They were murdered because of me! I got them all killed because I made a mistake."

The heat from Derain's eyes pierced the room and even Mr. Leon felt the need to take a step back. A dangerous man indeed.

"Where can I find them?"

Mr. Leon chuckled lightly. "First, we must talk about what you are going to do for me."

Derain half-lidded his eyes. His shoulders straightened as he slowly drew in a deep breath to regain control of himself. "Of course. My apologies."

***

Captain Kaplean settled himself in the comfort of his personal runner for the ride back to the shuttle. Mr. Alvarez was at the wheel and he had closed the privacy shield. As the windows tinted to opaque, the Captain pulled out of his data pad. He studied the files Ms. Shimada had compiled for him regarding Mr. Leon, but the man was an enigma.

There was a dearth of information on his early life, and little else. Until suddenly, ages later he resurfaces running a multi-system shipping industry. Sightings of the man had been recorded on completely different planets at roughly the same time, but there were no photos of him on file.

Even the pictures that the Captain had attempted to take were blank. Mr. Leon had obviously taken to wearing a 'shine'. That damnable technology. It prevented recordings and left just a brightly lit image with enough intensity to burn the lenses.

As mysterious as Mr. Leon was, he had been very helpful. He verified that a merchant ship named the Matilda claimed the salvage on the pirate corsair, the Garuda. He had also confirmed that a bounty hunter named Derain Tiwi used to fly with that freighter.

His communications officer, Ms. Shimada, also discovered that a recently freed revolutionary, Anton Roane, traveled on the Matilda before the police action on Timmony Bay. But just as the pieces were beginning to fit together, they flew off into entirely different directions. Never mind the latest news that the Independence had disappeared after its delivery to Nowhere.

Still, it was better to have too many leads than none. A person could work with that.

✳✳✳

Derain slowly set the stack of books he had taken from his grandfather's home onto the first book his grandfather had given him, the Book of Five Rings by Miyamoto Musashi. It had been a gift after his first stint in juvenile detention. Derain smiled at the memory.

"Read this!" his grandfather had exhorted him. "Take it to heart. It may save your life."

And it had. He had learned to control his anger and put that energy into more constructive uses. He had learned to use his skills and passions to get ahead in the life he chose. He could never thank his grandfather enough for believing in him after the rest of the family had turned their backs.

Derain clicked into his harness and brought up his ship's systems. Mr. Leon mentioned offhandedly that the Consortium might have left someone behind to track him and Derain was positive someone had tailed from the office building. He ran the ship through its preflight check. Best to be prepared. He switched on the comm, "Waratah to tower, Waratah to tower. Requesting permission for take-off."

He thought back to the last part of his conversation with Mr. Leon. The price for the information was the head of a woman called Dr. Judith Wyeth. That wasn't much to go on, but he had worked with less on other jobs. Of course, now that he knew where that mystery ship was, he was left with a choice.

"A simple choice really, Mr. Tiwi," the man had said to him. "Do you run to save your friend, or do you run to avenge your family? Do you fly for love or do you fly for rage?"

That smarmy smirk on his face, as if he knew the answer before Derain did, still irked him. But the difficult question remained, "Do I fly for love or do I fly for revenge?"

The comm interrupted his debate, "Tower to Waratah, tower to Waratah. You are clear for take-off."

fourteen

The Female Smuggler

"Galena, do you have a clue what the hell is going on?" Jacquie asked into the stunned silence.

Galena looked around in confusion, "I have absolutely no idea, Captain."

Another genorg approached the one on stage and whispered something into her ear. After she nodded, the genorg shouted, "Captain Jacquotte Delahaye? Are you in here? Is there a Captain Delahaye here?"

Jacquie tentatively raised her hand. The genorg who had whispered to the one on stage waved for a couple of armed genorgs to follow her and moved toward Jacquie. Jacquie slowly raised both her hands and Galena followed suit. The genorg in charge flicked her fingers at them and

Jon Gray Lang

waved them toward the exit. Jacquie slowly got up and Galena followed her out. As soon as Galena made it to the door, two of the genorgs stopped her and tied her hands together. She watched as Jacquie was led off around a corner.

"You. Follow me," muttered a young genorg miner, who yanked the restraints tight around Galena's wrists.

The battle on board the station continued with random bursts of gunfire erupting in the distance. Galena was led past teams of genorgs who held their rifles inexpertly over the crowds of station people. "What's going on here?" She received a firm jerk on her wrist restraints in answer.

Eventually, they came up to a lift. She stood there patiently trying to understand what was happening. Galena held her identity close to the chest. She didn't want to endanger herself or the Captain by accident. The lift doors parted and the woman holding her shoulder pushed her forward.

***

Jacquie glanced in both directions as she followed the genorg down the hallway, flanked by two more genorgs who guarded her steps. She looked over her shoulder and watched as Galena was shackled and led off in a different direction.

"What do you want from me?"

Her captors ignored her. They were all quite focused on getting her somewhere in a hurry. But where? What were they doing with the station? And most importantly, what did they want with her and Galena?

Anger tinged her words, "Could you at least let me know where we're going?"

All she got in response was a push from behind. The other two guards who kept their eyes on Jacquie spoke not a word.

The loud crack of a shot echoed in the hall as blood erupted from the genorg to her left.

"Go!" screamed the genorg on her right who began firing sporadically down the hallway. The third genorg jumped in front of Jacquie and yanked her forward. She dragged her down a hall in the administration section of the station and pushed her against the wall near a beaten metal door. The genorg hammered on the door then bolted to join her hard-pressed companions.

"Enter," barked a voice from the other side.

The sporadic gunfire grew louder by the minute. As the door swung open, a genorg guard pulled her in then shouldered past her. The door slammed shut with a heavy clank.

As Jacquie stumbled in, she spied a genorg in each of the back corners of the room while a third one sat behind a scarred industrial desk.

"Take a seat Captain Delahaye," commanded the genorg behind the desk.

Jacquie flopped into a seat, "You've got me at a disadvantage. Who might you be?"

"My registry is Tau-SA43."

Jacquie relaxed perceptibly. This stank of a negotiation and negotiations were part of her everyday business. Her lips curled into a humorless smile as she appraised the woman who sat across from her. She ignored the two in the back and tuned out the ongoing firefight in the hallway. This meeting was the important part and she had some say in it. The gun battle outside, not so much. She slid back into her chair and threw a leg over the armrest. The genorg quirked at Jacquie's lazy catlike posture.

An explosion shook the office walls and the genorgs flinched in surprise. Jacquie, on the other hand, steepled her fingers as dust fell from the ceiling, "You obviously need something from me. Tell me, what can the captain of a merchant ship, of one of the many captains on this station, possibly do for you and yours?"

Tau-SA43 smiled, "We had heard that you were astute and quick to the point. To the point then." She pulled a data pad from under the desk, "We have need of your vessel to move cargo to an undisclosed location."

"Undisclosed?"

"Yes, undisclosed."

"Why undisclosed? I'd need some sort of destination to get through the jump gate."

"Part of the cargo itself will explain where it is to be taken, but you will need to make two separate deliveries," replied Tau-SA34. "Neither of the shipments are very large."

"Two ports and no idea where they are?" Jacquie crossed her arms, "I'd love to help, but I've got other plans..."

"You are searching for a lost friend, yes?"

Jacquie's cheeks flushed with anger.

"Don't misunderstand me, Captain. You have no choice in this matter." Tau's face grew dark, "Either you fly for us or we take your ship."

"Over my dead body!"

The genorg ignored that outburst and continued, "However, if you'll comply with our request, we may help you search for your friend."

Jacquie leaned forward and placed her hands flat on the desk, "Well... that's going to cost you double." She fell back into the chair and started counting on her fingers, "Let's see, there is the cost of leasing space on my ship, the fuel costs for two cargo drops, import and export fees, not to mention docking fees for these 'unknown destinations'. What's more, since I don't know where we're going, I can only calculate half of this." She put on her best shit-eating grin, "Even with my life on the line, I'd have to charge you top mazuma. Now, I can see that this may come as a surprise, but you have me backed into a corner. So, even if I wanted to help, you couldn't afford it."

Tau-SA43 bestowed an indulgent smile, "They should add wily to your records, Captain Delahaye. But you are quite correct, we do have you 'in a corner', as you put it. However, we do understand that running a business such as yours in today's circumstances can be expensive and difficult."

Jacquie's eyes grew huge at the amount of mazuma that Tau-SA43 began piling in front of her. Even calculating out to the most expensive rates, this would get her further ahead than she had hoped. If these were simple cargo shipments with quick drop-offs, all the better.

As Tau-SA43 placed the last bundle of mazuma down on the desk, she was surprised at the excitement written across Jacquie's face. "Will this do, Captain?"

"Oh yes. This will do handsomely." Then Jacquie interjected, "What about the woman who was with me? I need her. I can't crew my ship alone."

Tau's eyes widened at the level of concern exhibited on the face of this natural-born woman.

***

The ride in the lift was quiet. Galena stood in the dead center of the elevator faced by the three genorgs who accompanied her. The lift wasn't quite as spacious as some of the ones used for moving cargo, but it was still plenty large.

'*We must be heading back to the ship berth section of the station*,' Galena thought. '*Were they going to space her? Were they going to put her on some ship and permanently separate her from Jacquie?*

She watched intently as the light for each floor lit up above the doors. Then suddenly the elevator settled. The genorg guards glanced at each other as a loud ding sounded, and the lift doors opened. The one in the middle shifted and Galena could see down the hall.

"Take cover!" shouted Galena.

She leapt forward and, with both wrists, struck the rifle out of the guard's hands. She raised her shoulder and shoved the now disarmed genorg into the wall.

Gunfire poured into the lift from outside and the genorg she had slammed into was hit multiple times. The guard closest to the control panel pulled the trigger on her rifle, but nothing happened. There was a cry from the hallway and two station security personnel hurled themselves into the lift. The genorg at the control panel was struck by a stray round and spun in place before her body dropped to the floor. A large man from security shoved the other genorg into the back wall. The doors shut and the lift continued its journey upwards.

Galena dropped to her knees and avoided the rifle butt that swung toward her back. As it crashed into the wall, she slammed her head into the stomach of the security woman who had swung it. The woman fell backward as an "oof" exploded from her.

Jon Gray Lang

With a grunt, the male security guard dragged his knife along the throat of the genorg he held trapped against the wall. Blood sluiced out and sprayed across the lift. Galena dropped to her back and pushed off the floor as the woman dropped the rifle butt where her head should've been. She bounced into the woman and rolled to the side. The woman fell back and obstructed the strike from the burly male. Galena hopped to her knees, pushed off the deck, and crashed into his ribs. He bounced off the lift wall and went down cold. Galena rolled up and leapt to her feet. The lift dinged once more and the doors parted. Standing before Galena were four more armed genorgs who kept their rifles trained on her.

Galena half smiled and shrugged, "We ran into some interference on the way up." She slowly stepped out amongst the others and waited. "Well? Which way am I supposed to go?"

One of the women pointed to the left with the rifle's barrel. The Lieutenant nodded with a half-grin and headed off in that direction followed by another armed genorg. She heard-more-than-saw the two security personnel being dragged out of the lift.

A large warehouse area with shipping containers stacked to the ceiling now surrounded her. Genorgs busily piled crates onto loaders and drove them off in different directions. From appearances, it looked as though the warehouse was being systematically stripped of its contents.

"Wait a minute." Galena stopped and turned to face the woman closest to her, "Are you guys robbing this place?"

***

Once the negotiation ended, they led Jacquie out of the office. The battle for the station seemed to be winding down as there were fewer bursts of gunfire in the distance. Jacquie kept checking to make sure the mazuma she had been given was still on her. Everything about that meeting had been surreal.

On the way to the lift at the end of the hall, Jacquie passed an old friend of hers, Captain Jibwe. He gave her a little wave as he was directed into the office she had just vacated. Her brow wrinkled in thought as a genorg directed her onto the lift, depressed a floor number button and then stepped back into the hall.

When the lift stopped and the doors parted at its destination, another armed genorg stood there waiting for her. As she disembarked, a group of genorg miners moved past her and rode the lift back down. Jacquie looked around and came to the realization that she was in the medical branch of the station. She watched lines of genorgs crawl inside open med tubes while other genorgs loaded the med tubes into huge crates. Eventually, these crates were stacked onto loaders and driven off toward the hangars.

Jon Gray Lang

"This way please," ordered the genorg.

Jacquie glanced over at her, "Quite an operation you've got here. Planning for a mass exodus or something?"

"The future can never be truly known."

"Best to be prepared for anything then, right?"

They continued on until they boarded another lift and rode it further up in the station. Her guide barely spoke, so Jacquie finally gave up trying to talk to her. She focused instead on her greatest concerns. She didn't know what condition Galena might be in and had no idea where to find her.

She hadn't expected this level of cooperation amongst the genorgs. They were coordinated, well-armed, and had taken over this station quickly with little trouble. They were obviously working toward some sort of goal and by the looks of it, they had outlined an escape plan too.

Jacquie continued following the genorg and mulling the information over in her mind. She ceased paying attention to where they were taking her when the genorg abruptly stopped. Jacquie looked up and was startled to see a line of crates being loaded into the cargo bay of her ship, the Matilda. She looked around, but she didn't see Galena anywhere.

The genorg stated, "Here is your ship. Have a pleasant trip."

"Wait! What about my copilot?" Jacquie grabbed the arm of the genorg as she about-faced, "Where is she?"

The genorg just pointed at the Matilda and said, "Bridge." She was joined by two others, then quickly walked away. Jacquie rotated between watching them depart and watching her ship being loaded. She shook her head and turned toward the Matilda.

***

The genorgs had locked Galena on the bridge of the Matilda. Unfortunately, she was forced to share her confinement with an incredibly annoying man who refused to keep his roaming hands to himself. Her captors said he was important. She hoped he might recover from having his head bounced off the comm station. Only time would tell.

Galena caught a brief glimpse of the Captain through the bow port. Jacquie was led to the ship, and as she entered the cargo bay, Galena lost sight of her.

Galena crossed her arms and slumped into the pilot's seat. The cargo bay was crawling with her sisters and she couldn't even use the comm. She would just have to wait until Jacq made her way up here.

It had been interesting to watch the loaders as they lined up and dropped crates for teams of genorgs to stow onto the various ships berthed at this end of the station. If this was happening to all the merchant vessels, this station could veritably be emptied of its contents. That would be one slick operation, if that was their plan.

She stood back up and watched the last of the loaders exit the cargo bay. The Matilda shook as the cargo bay doors trundled closed. It took forever before the hatch to the bridge was unlocked and Jacquie peeked inside.

"Galena? You in here?"

A happy sigh escaped the Lieutenant as she replied, "Yes. I am here, Captain! And am I glad to see you."

They collapsed into an embrace as they both sat down. For a long moment, they just stared at each other. Jacquie looked the same as she had at the Temptation. Galena, on the other hand, looked disheveled and slightly haggard.

"What happened to you?" they both asked simultaneously. Shared smiles and giggles broke the tension.

"You first," said the Lieutenant.

Jacquie touched Galena's face along a scratch lined with crusted blood, "No. What happened to you?"

Galena brought her hand up and took Jacquie's, "Oh you know. I got bored during a ride in the lift and had some fun. That didn't seem to agree with the powers that be, so I was locked in here and then you arrived." Galena's head tilted as she asked, "How about you?"

Jacquie smirked at Galena's levity, '*She acts more human every day. Maybe we're rubbing off on her?*' But she managed to keep a straight face and replied, "Nothing as exciting as your day." Her hand slipped from Galena's grasp and fell into her lap. "I negotiated a couple of new shipments at an exorbitant profit for us. That's about it."

Galena pursed her lips, "Um, while you were busy negotiating, did you see anything out of the ordinary?"

"Why? Did you?"

Galena's eyes lit up, "I sure did. I just want to know if I missed anything else happening out there."

Jacquie leaned in toward her, "Your sisters were hopping into med tubes that were then loaded into crates. Those crates were being loaded onto just about every ship on this end of the dock. I figure the same must be happening across the station." Her brow wrinkled in thought, "But there are a lot more crates than I expected for the number of genorgs."

Galena's face brightened, "Aah, that explains it. I was having the same quandary."

"What do you mean?" asked Jacquie.

"Well, I was taken through the warehouse section." She leaned in a little closer, "And they were stripping it. Anything and everything was being tossed into shipping crates and then loaded onto ships."

Jon Gray Lang

Their eyes lit up as they said in unison, "It's a robbery! A massive heist!"

The two women burst into peals of laughter. Whoever had set this up was going to make a lot of enemies. That is, if anyone ever figured out who had set the whole thing up. Using the station's mazuma to pay off all the ship captains at exorbitant rates would keep most of them quiet. Dropping the cargo all across Consortium space would make it nearly impossible to track. And using genorgs as the muscle made it that much more difficult to point fingers at who was responsible. The victims in this situation were going to have a tough time of it.

As their laughter died down, Galena looked up at the pilot's visor hanging above her head. Sadness welled up inside the center of her chest. She rolled her head to look in the Captain's direction, "I miss her laughter, Jacq. I miss Lu."

Jacquie grew somber. "Me, too," she sighed. "They said they might be able to help search for her after we make two deliveries."

Silence hung between them until Galena asked, "Two shipments? Where are we headed to anyway?"

"I don't know. Tau-SA43 gave me some cryptic remark that 'the cargo would tell me'. But I have no idea what she was talking about." Jacquie glanced over to the comm station and noticed a pair of legs sticking out from underneath it. "What's that?"

Galena's face took on a pained look, "I think that may be the cargo she was talking about."

fifteen

Forever

Luli's eyes fluttered and then squinted against the glare. All she could see was light. Her eyes refused to compensate. She blinked a handful of times, but the brightness didn't fade. She twisted her head from side to side, but she couldn't escape the glare. A tiny moan escaped her lips.

"Ms. Qing," said a voice from off to the side. "It is good to have you back."

She mumbled in response, "Back? Did I go somewhere?"

"Oh yes, Ms. Qing," the voice replied. "You died."

There was a catch in her throat as she whispered, "I saw the Major. Was... was he coming for me?"

The man's voice chuckled as he

wisecracked, "Well, the demon cannot have you yet."

His shadow blocked part of the light as his face drew closer to hers. It was still indistinct. What was wrong with her eyes?

He whispered, "I still need what you have. Then, maybe your Major can take you. Maybe then."

***

With a sudden gasp, Luli awoke. Forcefully, she peered all around her until the grip of fear around her heart lessened. The surrounding area was dim and the corners filled with shadows. Only one of the overhead lights was on. The monitoring station, with the broken one-way mirror, wasn't lit and remained unoccupied. She was alone in the room again and her eyes had finally adjusted.

She ran her system through a diagnostic and kept an eye out for anything out of the ordinary. She had wanted to escape, and something had provided it. What that something was, she wasn't entirely sure. It had forced her system into a complete shutdown she might not have returned from. Now that she was back, she hoped she could find the incriminating code in her operating system and reject it; to take back her body from those who had stolen it from her.

A list highlighted in red suddenly flashed onto her Head-Up Display in her eye. With a devious smile, Luli systematically removed the

Jon Gray Lang

code line by line with a thought. *'The future was now a little brighter than it had been, thank the Major.'* Her eyes were drawn to the small port in the room and out to the blackness of space.

She ran through the code and found the linchpin of the process. With a simple rewrite, she changed it to an alert if it was enacted. Now, it would feel like a tingly shock. She only had to make it look as if they had control of her chassis until she figured out where she was, what they wanted, and how to escape.

***

"Tell me, Ms. Qing," said the voice through the comm. "What do you remember of Earth?"

She looked around the room, and no sign existed of the brutes who had abducted her. She was alone except for that voice and something about it struck her as oddly familiar. There was a cadence to it that she recognized but couldn't quite identify.

"To be honest, I've never been there. My memories of Earth are only of a tiny blue dot in the blackness of space littered amongst the twinkling stars. All that I know of Earth is from stories, old pictures and movies. Do you remember Earth?"

"I have seen it, yes. But it was long ago, and my memories have faded. Does this make sense to you, Luli Qing? Do you feel that there is a hole in your mind when it comes to the Sol System?"

She thought about this for a while. A question asked could reveal almost as much as the answer. The point was in leading the questions toward the heart of the matter.

"A hole? No. I recall plenty of my time in the Sol System. Some good, some bad, but I remember enough."

"Have you ever thought of going back?" asked the voice.

'*The crux. There was the crux of the questions. What would someone like me, a deep spacer have that no passenger from a colony ship might have? A way back. A map back to Earth. But the last of us, the eight of us, had decided that no one should go back, so the map was broken into pieces.*' Each deep spacer committed only a part of the route to memory in an effort to protect the rest of humanity. They had all decided no one should return to see what had happened there.

She looked toward one of the monitoring cameras, "There is nothing to go back to. There is nothing left there."

"Are you so sure, Ms. Qing?"

"I am." Anger sparked her words, "I flew the last colony ship out of the Sol System and I saw it. I watched as the darkness enveloped the Sun and swallowed the Earth. I can still remember my fear that the wormhole wouldn't form in time to keep me and my passengers alive. Nothing but blackness is there now. The planets have all been snuffed out. The sun is dead and drained. There is no life there! There is nothing to go back to!"

"You are so quick to claim that there is nothing left, but are you sure? Perhaps your memories were tampered with? Might they have been altered?"

"You're right. They were tampered with, so humans could never go back. The only thing to find there now is death and if it finds you, it could follow you back here." She shivered at the memory.

The voice sighed into the comm, "Oh Ms. Qing. We humans should never have left our home system. We should not have scattered amongst the stars like rats leaving a sinking ship. We should have stayed and moved forward into our next step. You, of all of us, should understand this."

"Why would I understand anything like that?" she asked in confusion.

"You are one of the chosen ones, built to last in a universe that no longer needs you. You are an angel, a messenger for the people and like an angel, you are lesser than those selfsame people. But humanity still needs you and it is to complete a single task. We must make our way back home to reclaim it and become one with our next evolutionary step. We need your message to complete the prayer." The voice postulated, "To bring us to the next stage and join the Masters."

"That's why you murdered Vijay?

Did you kill Palba for this, too?" Tears spilled down her cheeks. "Are you going to butcher the rest of us for some bat shit crazy idea that you will become a God or something?"

The voice softly chuckled into the comm, "I cannot evolve. I, too, am but a messenger that is bound by the metals of the Sol System. Cursed to live until the message is heard."

She screamed into the air, "May the Major take you for a fool! There is nothing there! Darkness! Death! That is all you would find there. That is all anyone would find there!"

She stood up suddenly and a snarl curled her lips. She shuddered at the pain as her fists clenched and she stomped toward a single hanging camera. With a sudden leap, she knocked the camera out of its holding, and watched it smash against the floor. Her body was zapped with a fiery tingle and she allowed herself to fall to the decking.

"Ms. Qing. Ms. Qing," the voice admonished tartly. "You must learn to control your urges."

"I got you, sucker," she quietly muttered to herself. Her reboot had successfully locked out her captor's programming and she had tested it with this rash act. Even better, she finally had been able to peg that voice. It belonged to Jarl Moritsson, one-time partner for life of the long-dead Palba Lazano. "I've got you."

Jon Gray Lang

sixteen

High Speed Changer

Derain's departure from the surface of Aketi had been anything but routine. Traffic Control sounded nervous as they rushed to get him off-world. Considering what he had been told by both Thando and Mr. Leon, trouble was on the prowl so he kept an eye out.

The Waratah's flight path remained clear until it flew past the L4 Lagrange Point. His radar tracked a blip that came from the rubble trapped there before the tailing ship's signature was obscured by his shadow. Another ship broke off its orbit of the local moon as he cruised past it. Both radar signatures were tiny, but their heat readings were peculiar. Whenever there was a sudden burst of movement, their engine heat lit up the scope.

"They must be using dampers to

cancel it out." A dangerous smile spread across Derain's face, "Sloppy to use thrusters without the dampers set correctly. Damn sloppy. Those must be some green pirates to forget the proper method for quiet pursuit."

Derain set the coordinates of his ship to the jump gate and monitored their response. The two heat signatures that lit up his scope failed to keep a decent following distance. He revised his opinion; they must be a pair of planet-bound government shills.

It had been a long while since he'd had a run-in with these types. With his logged course on screen, he checked the timer to his destination. A dry chuckle echoed inside his helmet as he located the best place to waylay them. Even if there were more of them out there, they must want him alive. He didn't suffer from the same compunction. Yes, there was plenty of time. Plenty of time, indeed.

***

"Is that responder popping yet?" Barney shouted.

Anton winced at the volume, "The Cyclops is a small boat, Barney. Shouting isn't necessary."

"Well then, answer the question the first time I ask it!" Barney huffed back.

Anton fiddled with some settings on

his data pad, then dropped it. He yanked off the covering over the yacht's hardware, hunkered down, and sorted through the wires until he found the bad connection. With a bit of a grin, he licked the end of the offending wire and reseated it into its slot. There wasn't a change until he blew onto one of the boards and dislodged whatever microbe of dust was blocking it's function.

"How about now?" Barney walked over holding a comm, "My contact at the tower says the Demetrius is requesting permission to depart. We need that responder back in operation now or all of this is for nothing!"

Anton bounced up and slapped at a setting on his data pad. A small light began to blink on the radar screen. His grin grew into a proud smile, "Well, it's working now. Go ahead and get permission to leave."

Barney rattled the request quickly into the comm and waited for confirmation. Once he got it, he waved Anton over to the pilot's seat and strapped himself down at the comm station. Anton popped the cover back on and hopped into the pilot's seat. He powered through the pre-flight procedures and felt the ship vibrate as the engines fired. With a quick nod from Barney, he backed the Cyclops slowly out of its berthing slot away from Reverie Station.

Barney flipped the responder signal to a separate frequency and tapped through the settings until he picked up the Demetrius's outgoing comms to the tower. A wicked smile of satisfaction lit up his face.

"... Station Control, Demetrius at taxiway Delta, ready to taxi," came statically through the comm.

"Demetrius, taxi to launch tube 78 Alpha..." came from the comm a minute later.

Barney crowed, "We've got them. They're using a wide frequency, so we'll need to keep relatively close. Close enough to get the signal, but not close enough to set them off. Got it?"

"Fly casual. Got it."

He didn't like the idea of Yannick Specht being trapped on that boat. But if these were the same goons that had nabbed Luli, they had to leave him there as bait. He just hoped nothing would happen to the guy.

They were given permission to depart. He took the Cyclops out of the station and into normal space. The Demetrius was set for a standard course to the jump gate, so he kept the yacht on the periphery of the responder's signal. Barney remained focused on the comm and listened for any travel plans from their quarry. Once they knew where that boat was going, they could send a message via gate channels to both the Waratah and the Matilda.

Jump Gate Communications was what made the whole network function. The time delays for communications between planetary systems and their jump gates were almost as time-consuming as ship travel between the two. But communications between gates only took the same amount of time it took for a ship to travel through the connected wormhole. This allowed for a fast response from the military arm of the Consortium, but it also tracked the ebb and flow of goods needed for the free markets of the systems.

Due to its high usage between trade market representatives, the cost of sending and holding messages for other ships, merchant or otherwise, was minimal. When a ship arrived at a gate or went through one, messages could be sent and received, once their gate charge was processed.

This meant that a best-case scenario for the Cyclops would be that the Matilda and the Waratah would learn of their next destination within a handful of hours. If either ship was at a gate, they could meet up with them soon after. At worst, it could take a month or more for the information to reach them.

The main problem was that the process did leave a digital trail for someone else to follow. But they had all decided that, for the sake of Luli, they would chance it. Considering some of the heat they had experienced of late, everyone had their fingers crossed.

It was a long drawn out flight as they slowly neared the jump gate. A static burst signaled activation of the comm, "Demetrius requesting travel permit to the Ankara system. I repeat Demetrius requesting travel permit to the Ankara system."

Barney held his hand over the comm, and Anton strained to hear the jump gate's response.

"Demetrius, you have been granted travel access to the Ankara system. I repeat, Demetrius, you have been granted travel access to the Ankara system."

"Message received. Demetrius out."

"Are you setting the coordinates for the Ankara system?" Barney asked as he wrangled through the Jump Gate's mail system.

"Of course!" Anton angrily replied. "Have you sent that data message off to Jacquie and Derain?"

Barney just glared in response. Once they were within the proper range, Barney fired off the mail for the crew of the Matilda, then requested travel access to Ankara.

For the most part, the Ankara system was made up of gas giants that were being mined for fuel. There was a single planet in the system that could house life and it was covered in domes filled with the more leisurely pursuits. Considering the system, it was the most suitable destination.

"Let's hope this is an actual lead and we're not going off on some Gods forsaken wild goose chase," Barney muttered.

seventeen

God's Gonna Cut You Down

A grumble escaped the Captain as she stared at the pair of legs that stuck out past the edge of the comm station. It took a fair bit of effort, but she and Galena finally managed to drag the body out into the open. When Jacquie saw the face, her's wrinkled into a pained expression and she slumped backward into her seat.

"You know him?" Galena asked after seeing the Captain's expression.

Jacquie's lip pursed in derision, "Unfortunately, yes. He's a liar with an attitude problem, and a two-bit thief."

Jacquie stood up and grabbed his feet, "Come on. Help me get him down to sickbay."

The Lieutenant picked him up by the waist. The man was small in stature and didn't have a single hair on his head. He was developing quite the welt on his forehead where the comm had struck him. She didn't feel bad about it, though. They carried him into the lift and waited for the doors to close.

Jacquie felt a hand caress her backside. She smacked the hand away, barely noticing the smirk that spread across his face. "Just so you know, he's a bit grabby," Jacquie advised.

"Oh, I know. That's why he was face down on the decking," Galena replied.

Jacquie chuckled in understanding. "You've pegged him to a T. Keep reprimanding him then. Eventually, he might learn."

Galena forced a smile, "One can hope."

On the ride down to the first deck, Jacquie noticed that Galena looked a little paler than usual. The lift dinged and the doors parted open to the cargo bay. Once they maneuvered him out, it didn't take long to arrange his body into a med tube. The lid closed quietly. Doc registered that the tube was in use and slid over toward it on his track.

"Can you take a look at him, Doc?" asked Jacquie.

"Che tuu. Che tuu da!" Doc's voice chirped into the air.

Jacquie just rolled her eyes at him and stepped over to the medicine cabinets, "Yes, yes. I can see that you already are." She rifled through one of the drawers and pulled out a thermometer, "Hey

Galena, could you come over here? You look a little peaked to me."

As the words left her mouth, a preternaturally cold hand seized Jacquie's shoulder. She turned to see Galena staring at her with pitch-black eyes. With no time to react, Jacquie was shoved away from the cabinets and slammed against the side of a med tube. As she slid to the decking, the Lieutenant jumped on her.

Snarling and spitting like a soul possessed Galena wrestled the Captain down and sat on her arms. Jacquie struggled against her, but Galena's hands gripped her head and held it firmly in place. Jacquie was trapped and her struggles were to no avail. Dark viscous goo ran from the Lieutenant's eyes and formed tracks down her cheeks.

Galena's thumbs pulled the Captain's eyelids back and held them open. Jacquie struggled even more as the black sludge slid from Galena's face, poised to drip directly into her eyes.

The Lieutenant's voice hissed strangely through the sickbay, "Follow me to the very edge, Captain. Let go and fall into the abyss..."

With a resounding crunch, the Lieutenant's hands grew limp. Her body was yanked off Jacquie and smashed into the medicine cabinets like a ragdoll. Doc hovered over Jacquie with all of his arms extended. Jacquie blinked and shook from the adrenaline rush. She looked over at the Lieutenant who lay in a pool of her own blood.

Jon Gray Lang

Galena's eyes stared back unblinking, but they were crystal clear.

"Don te kuu ta lae!" Doc's voice rumbled.

"You got her back alright, Doc," Jacquie panted. "The debt is repaid indeed."

***

"I know it's you, Jarl," Luli growled from the decking. "It took me a while to figure it out, but you always had that damnable lilt in your voice."

A sardonic chuckle came over the comm before it went silent.

The fiery tingle disappeared from her nerve endings. She sat up slowly and dusted herself off. She surreptitiously looked around and there were only a couple of visible cameras left in the room. She scanned for heat sources and besides the obvious equipment, a couple of hot spots showed up on the ceiling. The whole set up was a little ramshackled. As she stood up, she caught a glimpse of a face through the hatch porthole. She threw a little curtsy and went back to her chair and took a seat.

As the hatch opened, she felt a tingle run through her nerve endings. She pretended to lock her muscles to maintain the ruse that she was still under his control. Her gaze riveted on him as the hatch opened and he stepped into the room.

Jon Gray Lang

Jarl Moritsson didn't look much different from the way she remembered him; older, grayer and a bit worn. He was still shorter and broader than she was, but his curly hair had grown longer; well, taller might be a better way to put it. He wore a string of memory cores around his neck and he clutched a small remote in his right hand. The hatch slid closed behind him.

"Hey, Jarl. I can't say that I'm happy to see you," said Luli. "You're looking a little haggard these days." Her mouth twisted, "So, how did it feel to take Palba's life? Did it feel good to watch the woman you love die by your hand? I can tell you that watching Vijay being butchered in front of me gives me nightmares."

Spittle flew from her mouth as she screamed, "What happened to you out there? Are you going to kill all of us for your idiotic crusade? How many of us are even left?"

His expression became a little pained at her words and he slowly came to a stop in the middle of the room. Her throat ached from the unspoken anger, so she just glared at him. He gazed back at her and watched as her tears caught in the ragged seams of her broken skin.

"Well?" she asked again, "How many of us are left?"

He moved away from her to pull a chair through the shattered one-way mirror of the monitoring booth. With very deliberate steps, he brought it over and set it down just out of her reach.

His hands came together in his lap as he gingerly slid into the chair and tightly clutched the small remote.

That familial warmth that she found repugnant filled his voice, "It is good to see you again, Luli. It has been a very long time since I last saw you or one of the others in person. So long, in fact, that a part of me still thinks of you all as my friends."

Five memory cores clinked against his chest. Since she was imprisoned and Jarl obviously still lived, that meant that there was only one other deep spacer left who might be free. A snarl escaped Luli as she struggled to keep herself from leaping toward him and wrapping her broken hands around his throat to choke the life out of him. What made it all the worse was how he sat there looking genuinely sad about it. Her cheeks colored from her efforts to restrain her impulses.

Jarl reached over and brushed the hair away from her damaged scalp. He frowned with concern and his hand dropped back into his lap. "I am sorry that your skin was repaired so clumsily. It is not something that we generally bother with for the messengers. Well, all of them, except you."

"You are different, Luli." The tiniest of smiles appeared on his face then disappeared. "You have always been different, haven't you? Different from the rest of us, anyway. Something about the way you were assembled."

"Not as easy to strip me of my soul is it?"

Jon Gray Lang

"It's funny that you should say it that way," he smiled sardonically. "Palba and I used to discuss the existence of such a thing. She did not believe in spirits while I did."

Luli gritted her teeth, "Is that why you murdered her?"

He replied sharply, "Once she saw the truth of life, she gave hers willingly. But I do miss her. This journey is hard on a being's soul, especially one that is lonely."

"Willingly? I don't believe you. I... I can't believe you." Luli cried, "Palba was no believer. Hard, cold facts and nothing else. That was her way." She felt the fiery tingle cross her face as it centered around her lips. Now would she have to hold her tongue still?

A broad smile blossomed on Jarl's face, "She was very much that way, it is true. But it was what we found together that changed her mind and let our journey truly begin."

Slowly he rose to his feet and began to pace. Luli struggled to sit still and stare straight ahead as he continued, "We traveled together for years... for as long I can remember. We grew tired with the rest of humanity in Consortium space. We both hungered for new experiences, new places."

He turned toward her, "We pooled our resources and purchased an old colony ship that still had an intact FTL apparatus. It didn't technically work, but the repairs were simple enough. It cost us everything, but what is mazuma for if not

Jon Gray Lang

for dreams?"

He stepped over the broken camera lying on the decking. "At first, we initiated very small jumps, just to test her. After a few failed attempts and some fine-tuning, we were off. We traveled to systems unknown to us. We saw astronomical anomalies, yet, in the end, we discovered very little. But we were happy. As happy as we had been for many planet-bound generations."

"But still, we felt there was something missing." He stopped and stood in front of the small port in the wall, "And it slowly eroded us. We fought, and the happiness we'd had passed away into oblivion. But we continued to travel together. What else was there for us to do?"

An unbridled sense of wonder filled his eyes, "And that is when we found her."

The tingle disappeared from Luli's face. She let her jaw sag before she asked, "Her?"

Jarl walked over and rested his hand against the pitted hull of the ship, "Her... the Polypheme. This very ship that I now pass my days in. I don't think I've actually been off-board in many years."

As far as Luli could tell, this ship was just a rusting hulk of space trash that had been left to rot. As she looked around and tried to digest this, she felt his eyes on her. A fever burned in those eyes; the very heat of it scorched her.

"This is no ordinary vessel, Luli. No ordinary stripped hulk that even a salvage crew would ignore." Jarl cupped her chin, so he could stare deeply into her eyes, "She has secrets, Ms. Qing. Secrets she wants to share. And if you're special, she will share them with you as she did with Palba and finally me."

His hand dropped from her chin. "Secrets. You can hear them, see them and taste them when you're just on the edge of sleep. They come to you when you least expect it and they show you things. The truth, the plan, the path for us all."

"They?" Luli asked as she broke his gaze.

But he didn't hear her. He continued on his diatribe, "They showed Palba first. They told her that the way home would lead us back to the Eden mentioned in the ancient stories. She tried to escape the truth, but they hounded her to accept it. She begged me to leave this place, but I couldn't bring myself to. They kept me here, so she couldn't escape their message."

He turned back toward Luli, "It is for her that I am still here. It is because of Palba that I continue the work that she started."

"What was the message you ask?" he pondered out loud as Luli looked on in confusion. "It was terribly simple. Find the way home and begin the trek back. But only one messenger could know the whole map and that was the problem."

Vehemently, he turned toward her, "We, the last of the deep spacers, sundered that map! So, it was our curse that only one of us can bear the whole of it, will bear the wholeness of it. And with that knowledge rattling around in her mind, Palba pried the memory core out of her own skull and left it for me to find!"

Anger radiated from him, "And who had said we should break the star charts apart so that none of us could go back? Who was the last of us to leave Eden with her mouth full of lies?" He stabbed her in the chest with his index finger, "Luli Qing. You are why this is the only path left for us. You are why my sweet Palba took her life. Because she knew that she was not the one to know the way."

His fingers stroked the necklace of memory cores that encircled his neck, "All of these memories were taken so that the route back to the Eden of our species could be found. And they were taken in your name, for your decision."

"I have nothing to do with your sick dreams," Luli spit back. "Do not blame me for your actions."

Jarl's mouth twisted into a knot as he jabbed a button on the remote. Luli's body was struck by a tingle that hit all of her nerve endings, so she remained still. Jarl turned away from her and surprise was written across his face.

His arms went wide, "Can you see them? The Masters are all around us!" He threw his head back, "They bless us with their presence!"

Luli felt her stomach tie itself in knots while dark color spectrums streamed across the corners of her vision. The very air stank of molten copper and rotting fruit. Her eyes clamped shut as wave after wave of nausea struck her. She clenched her stomach muscles to keep from losing the little food she had eaten over the past few days. The stench grew stronger. The nutty scent of insect carapaces drying on a hot muggy day permeated her mind.

'Gods! Are we jumping?' sprang to her mind as she tried to shut her systems down.

The crashing sound of a gong penetrated her mind and reverberated to the very center of her being. Like shadows cast from who knew where, slug-like beings grew from the floor and formed a circle in the center of the room. Her body bonelessly slid out of the chair.

"What have you done to me, Jarl?

Jarl cried out in elation and giggled with the laughter only madmen can conjure. His frame twitched through the steps of a jig as the entities around him faded in and out of existence. Luli struggled to make sense of what she was seeing until her system went dark.

eighteen

Le Disko

The two ships tailing the Waratah hadn't made any sudden moves as they kept far to the rear. A betting man might think they'd hold off their attack until they got closer to the jump gate since they most likely were in the employ of one of the military arms of the government.

But Derain wasn't a betting man. He was a man who learned his quarry's behavior, so he could limit their options down to a handful of responses and trap them at their own game. From the little that he was able to glean, it seemed as if they wanted to keep this quiet and out of sight of the jump gate response ships. There must be a trap set for him in the very near future.

The best point for him to be waylaid would be out past the fifth planet in the system.

The planet's outer stratosphere would gum up his readings on any ship that might be lying in wait and he wouldn't be able to catch any non-direct comm chatter in time. He shouldn't even see it coming.

The two radar signatures behind him screamed short-range light fighters. That meant that there must be an advance drop fighter carrier up ahead with a standard accompaniment of four of the lightships. With the two behind him and two more ahead with the carrier itself, they had him outnumbered. They had him outgunned as well.

However, he knew it was a trap. He didn't have to play by their rules, and he had an assortment of tricks that wouldn't be in their books. Never mind the fact that Barney had made some changes to the Waratah after their second run-in with a Consortium cruiser.

One important thing in any fight is communication. Derain got out of the pilot's seat and floated over to the storage cabinets near the airlock hatch. He carefully pulled out a large cylindrical tube and shut the cabinet. The second most important thing is information, as in knowing what to expect. He stepped back over to the console and checked the existing loaded inventory. Lastly, and truly the most important, was coming out ahead.

He moved back to the benches that ran the length of the rear of his ship. After removing the cushions, Derain pulled the lid off the storage unit underneath and rummaged around until he freed an incredibly thick, oblong barrel. After the bench was put back together, he produced a heavy tripod from another cabinet. Lastly, he reached in and brought out the firing mechanism and the power cable to the whole assembly.

It took some time to put together the portable rail gun assembly and bolt it into the decking. The weapon's interface read a full charge once it was connected. As he pulled out a large magazine and clapped it into place, the weapon registered as loaded. His hands rested on his hips while he surveyed everything before him. Now it all depended on one thing and she was a fickle mistress. Timing. Everything came down to timing.

***

"Wolf Two to Wolf Three. You copy?" asked the pilot of one of the pursuit ships.

So far, tailing the Waratah had been uneventful. Her pilot had chosen a standard flight pattern to the jump gate with little to no variance. Wolf Two snorted at the thought. Everything read as an easy takedown on whoever this guy was. She didn't know why her commander wanted him, nor did she care.

Isa's comm lit up, "Wolf Three to Wolf Two. Coming up on the rendezvous point. You ready for the takedown? Oh shi...!"

"Wolf Two to Wolf Three. Repeat? Wolf Two to..." She toggled the switch, but the comm channels were down.

She switched over to the wide broadcast to sync up to the carrier, but something was blocking it. She glanced out the starboard side and watched her wingman drift off course. "What the hell are you doing, Kofi?"

***

Derain whistled a little ditty as he pulled back the breach on the railgun that he had bolted to the decking. The rear hatch to his ship was open to the void so that his view remained unobstructed. The confounder he had pushed out seemed to be functioning properly. He sighted in on the other ship still tailing him and locked onto the cockpit. As he slowly released a pent-up breath, he squeezed the trigger. The heavy round exited the barrel and shot its way toward the enemy ship. He swung the hatch closed and strapped himself back into the pilot seat.

***

Wolf Two watched as her wingman drifted farther out and settled into a lazy circle, "Damn it! What are you doing?" Had she missed something?

Isa jerked as something smashed through her canopy. The Head-Up Display exploded, and fragments ricocheted all over the cockpit. The projectile slammed into her head and bounced it off the back of the headrest. Pieces of her helmet followed the slug into her skull and out through the back of the seat. Her body slumped to the side and her foot slipped against the pedal for the attitude jets. The slight turn caused her arm to rest against the stick. Her light fighter began a slow and wide turn out into the darkness of space.

***

Derain checked his radar display and watched as the two fighters slowly circled outward from his present trajectory. He tried to check ahead, but the moon was blocking the other ship's signatures. He nervously tapped his fingers against the console. The most dangerous part of the plan lay ahead. If either of the pursuit ships had been able to get a comm off to the carrier, they had him. If they hadn't, then he still had a chance.

He ran through his weapons inventory. Due to their function as advance dropships, the bow on a small carrier was covered in heavy plating. Consequently, they were most vulnerable to damage in the rear. He had maneuverability on his side against the carrier, but the light fighters had an advantage on him.

He tapped at the faceplate of his helmet. With a flick of a switch, he dropped the ship's dampers in place. With a couple taps at the attitude jets, his forward momentum slowed tremendously. The Waratah coasted toward the moon until he brought it to a full stop near the surface.

On this side of the moon, his ship shone as a bright spot on the surface. His hope was that the angle the other ship took would keep him in the dark for as long as possible. Derain crossed his fingers and settled down to wait.

***

Scanner Technician Rodriguez flinched in reaction to the display on his screen. Wolf Two and Three shot past the carrier's position on the other side of the moon.

He tracked them for a moment before he declared, "Um, sir? Both of our pursuit craft have shot past our position."

Commander Tong glanced over to him, "Any sight of the quarry?"

"No sighting of the Waratah, sir," replied Technician Rodriguez.

"Ms. Hatch? Please hail them. Find out what's going on."

"Sir, yes sir." The Communications Officer tried to contact the fighters through multiple frequencies. "There appears to be some interference, sir. I am unable to get through."

"Probably the moon mucking up the comm," answered the Commander. "Helm, take us out past the curve."

Jon Gray Lang

"Sir, yes sir."

Commander Tong switched his comm to the launch bay, "Launch Wolf Four. Trajectory is..." He turned to Mr. Rodriguez, "Which ship is closer?"

"That would be Wolf Two, sir."

The Commander toggled the comm back on, "Trajectory is Wolf Two."

Wolf Four shot past the edge of the moon and accelerated into a turn toward the closest of the lost light fighters. It was a matter of minutes for the small carrier, CVA-1, to pass the edge of the moon. Officer Hatch tried to raise the light fighters, but again to no avail.

Ms. Hatch called out, "Sir? I think the comms are being jammed."

An anomaly appeared out of the darkness on Technician Rodriguez's display. He forced the scan to run a tight beam on it, but the image came back muddled. "I think I found the device jamming the signal. It's to the starboard side."

"Send the vectoring to the gunnery," ordered Commander Tong. "Everyone, keep sharp. The waters are bloodied. Our prey is more of a shark than we anticipated."

***

When the third light fighter shot by in pursuit of its partners, Derain sighted down his targeting system. He was easily able to get a lock on the carrier as it came out past the edge of the moon. They had launched only one of the remaining light fighters. The other was still attached to its launch tube.

A wicked grin crossed his face as he honed in on the two separate targets. With a tingling sense of anticipation, he primed the tubes and pressed the launch buttons in quick succession. As the missiles burst from his ship, Derain brought the engines up and headed toward the carrier.

***

"Shots are away," announced Gunnery Visser.

"Very good. Keep us informed, Gunnery," said the Commander.

"Sir. Yes sir," he replied as he tracked his shots on the display screen.

A small fiery blossom flashed on the starboard side of the main viewport. Then the skies went dark. Suddenly the decking of the ship buckled beneath the feet of the bridge crew. The small carrier rocked forward and tilted to starboard. Alarms blared all over the ship and the comm was littered with chatter.

"Target ship coming up from the rear!" yelled, Rodriguez, the Scanner Technician.

Commander Tong commed to the hangar team, "Launch Wolf One! I repeat, launch

Wolf One!"

"Sir!" shouted Officer Hatch, "Damage Control states that the starboard aft engines have sustained an explosion. They are trying to bring the fire under control!"

The comm chimed back, "Wolf One is gone, sir. It was a direct hit. She's gone!"

Commander Tong ordered Mr. Visser, "Track that ship and knock it out of the sky!"

Officer Pinch declared, "Sir. The moon's gravity is starting to affect our directional controls and we are losing altitude."

"Hatch! Get Damage Control on those engine repairs now!" screamed the Commander. "Pinch, hit the attitude jets to pull us out of this spiral!"

Communications Officer Hatch affirmed, "Wolf Four has caught up to Wolf Two, but the pilot is dead. He is swinging back around."

***

The Waratah rocketed toward the small carrier and Derain adjusted the course toward the starboard side. He had watched the ship list and judged that the ship's attitude jets would be employed to pull it out of the spiral, "Heat-seekers away." His grin grew a tiny bit wider as the flames from the missiles streaked across the night sky.

***

Jon Gray Lang

Gunnery Visser ran through his scanners searching for any radar signature of the ship that was tearing their vessel apart. He cursed loudly at the giant blind spot along the rear of this model of carrier ship. The extreme heat from the engines obscured any temperature and light readings, not to mention the residual radioactivity. The best chance he had was to throw his mazuma to Lady Luck. Quickly, he selected three random targets in the center of the blind and released a salvo... and crossed his fingers.

"Shots away," stated the Gunnery. The carrier shuddered from a strong impact on the starboard side. "It's not our day," the officer muttered under his breath.

"Starboard attitude jets assembly destroyed," Officer Hatch relayed. "Wolf Four should be back in 5 minutes."

"Too late to help us," cursed the Commander. "Mr. Pinch, drop the dampers and pour on the power. Let's see if we can shunt out some of that propulsion and pull in some reverse movement. At least to slow us down."

"Sir! Yes, sir!"

***

Derain watched in satisfaction as the shield dampers began to drop over the engines. The dampers were gigantic metal shields designed to absorb the heat from the engine output and also to block the light source from scanners. Angled just right, they could be used to bounce the propulsive forces in the reverse direction of the engines themselves. If he had been in the same position, he would have tried the same thing. But since he was expecting it, he almost felt guilty about the salvo of unguided rockets he already had launched at the massive hinge that moved the damper in the first place.

The rockets burst like fiery flowers along the inner joint of the hinge. The giant damper's movement ground to a halt as the port engines exploded to life on the small carrier. The spin of the ship increased and its angle toward the moon became more pronounced. There were few options left for the carrier as it slipped into the moon's gravity, soon to smash against the surface.

Derain cut the power to his engines and rode the slingshot reaction out toward the jump gate. He arose from the pilot seat and casually opened the ship's hatch to drop another confounder out into the moon's orbit. That should cut communications between the last fighter and its home carrier, and hopefully any passersby in the meantime. He hunkered down behind the railgun and loaded in another round.

The use of his last option was entirely dependent on what the last light fighter pilot did in response to discovering his mother ship had crashed onto the moon's surface. The best-case scenario would be for the pilot to make his way to the jump gate due to the fuel restrictions of the craft itself. "But people didn't always make the best decisions, did they?"

***

Wolf Four burned his thrusters at full to get back to his mother ship, but it was too late. The pilot watched as the carrier slammed into the surface of the small moon and the vessel cracked in half from the impact. Portions of the hull's shielding broke off and skittered across the surface. Small explosions flared up along the rupture in the hull only to be snuffed out as the internal atmosphere of the ship was depleted.

His fist slammed into the dashboard of the cockpit. His fuel levels were too low to make it back to Aketi. He should be able to make it to the jump gate with the reserves, though. A small fire caught his eye. He looked down at his scanner and read a heat signature as it rocketed away from the crash site.

"There you are, you bastard." His lips curled back into a scowl, "Kill my people? You'll join them before you get out of here."

The pilot smacked the attitude jets to swing the ship hard out and gunned his fighter into pursuit. That guy had taken out his wing and decimated his home carrier. He triangulated the target vessel's trajectory and his own to find the optimal cross point. Luckily, it wasn't far and the best way to catch up was a straight run at it. The maximum range for a missile lock was one hundred kilometers. That was still far enough away for chaff to cause it to miss.

He would have to get much closer. His fuel reading steadily dropped. His ability to get to the jump gate disappeared while he remained focused on his goal. As he slowly caught up to it, he could just make out the ship against the blackness of space. He snorted in satisfaction as the distance shrank. It was just a dropship! With the amount of damage it had left in its wake, he had expected something larger or more maneuverable. This kill would be easy.

A small object punctured through the plas-glass of his canopy. Before the pilot knew what hit him, he was being showered with broken shards of the canopy. The object had slammed into his faceplate and out through the back of his helmet. His body jerked from a burst of adrenaline, but the brain was already dead. The fuel reading on the ship continued to drop as it shot past the dropship with its rear hatch open. Wolf Four continued its burn out into the darkness of space.

***

The Waratah arced toward the jump gate. Derain had disassembled the rail gun and put it away before he radioed the jump gate tower with his request to leave the system. No red flags sprung up on his arrival and the personnel on the comm treated him as normally as they ever had. His best option was to appear as calm as possible.

While he waited for clearance to enter the wormhole, a chime went off in his helmet announcing new messages had been received. His eyebrows quirked as he shuffled through a handful of headlines that referred to genorg troubles on a mining colony and a trading station. One message, in particular, caught his eye. It was from the Cyclops. He pushed for retrieval and the message displayed across his helmet faceplate.

"We are tracking a lead to the Ankara system. Signed, A & B."

Derain smiled. He was glad that Anton had been able to sneak Barney onboard the Cyclops. It might piss off Jacq once she found out, but she stood by herself on the decision for his dismissal. For that reason alone, he was certain that the message sent out to the Matilda wouldn't have Barney's initial on it.

"Jump Gate Tower to the Waratah, please respond," came through the comm. "This is the Aken Jump Gate Tower to the Waratah, please respond."

"Waratah here. I repeat, Waratah here," Derain replied.

"Please state your destination."

The choice lay before him. He could go after the people who had butchered his family or he could try to help a friend. He no longer had a family. And friends? He didn't have many.

It had been a long time since Derain had visited the Ankara system. Though it was rich in gases and other rare resources, it was out on the fringes of the Consortium. Being out on the edge meant it also had a reputation of being a wild place. There was only a single planet with an actual surface suitable for building structures on and it was home to an underworld that ran some of the most debauched clubs in the whole of the Consortium. And that was saying a lot.

"Waratah requesting travel permit to Ankara system. I repeat, Waratah requesting travel permit to Ankara system."

There was a long pause before the tower replied, "Waratah, you have been granted travel access to the Ankara system. I repeat, Waratah, you have been granted travel access to the Ankara system."

The choice was made then, and something in him felt better for the decision.

"Message received. Waratah out."

nineteen

F**k It Man

Rex Leon sat across from his counterpart who ran their corporate office on Silk Road Station. He watched as the man dithered about in the background. Eventually, he came forward with two cups. He set one down in front of Rex and took one for himself. In unison, the pair of them sniffed at the tea as the steam wafted about their faces before they sat back and sighed deeply.

"It is good to see one of us in the flesh again," Mr. Leon said as he brought a small clay pot over to the desk.

As Rex took a sip, a contented smile settled on his lips. He set the cup back down. "It has been too long, my brother." He scratched at his temple thoughtfully, "Though technically you are physically closer to more of the brotherhood than

Jon Gray Lang

any of the rest of us."

"Touché, brother." Mr. Leon winked back, "Let's keep that detail under the wire, please. Even with the amount of anti-bug systems that we have running in this office, you never know when a new version will be built that there is no protection against."

Rex took another sip of his tea. "Of course. My apologies." He held the dainty cup out and admired the color of the tea liquor inside it, "This is an astoundingly excellent leaf. Is this from...?"

"Why yes, it is," Mr. Leon exclaimed. "It's the last parcel I have that is planet grown. From it, we've grafted a new strain that has been found to grow remarkably well in low gravity. We are all quite pleased with the success of the plant." He set his cup down and it clinked against the desktop, "In fact, we're into the third-generation growth and there haven't been any deficiencies detected as of yet."

"Oh, excellent news." Rex looked over the lip of the cup, "Would I perchance be able to abscond with some on my way out? It is hard to remain civilized in space without a good cup of tea."

"I could only guess," Mr. Leon replied. "But the answer is a resounding yes. See my secretary on your way out and he will have a packet waiting for you."

"Could you have it handed over to my bodyguard, Rosa Keri?" Rex requested. "Sometimes it is hard on the natural-borns to meet more than one of us at the same time."

"Oh, yes of course. How silly of me." Mr. Leon keyed the comm to his secretary and gave him the instructions regarding the package. Once he was done, he nodded at Rex, "Now that that is out of the way, we can finally discuss why you are here."

"I received the summons from the brotherhood, so here I am." Rex interlaced his fingers, "What was the dire need to see me directly?"

Mr. Leon set his tea down and placed his hands flat against the desktop. Under Mr. Leon's intense gaze, Rex suddenly felt as if thousands of eyes were tracking his every movement from across the desk.

It was a strange feeling, especially since he had never been on the receiving end of such scrutiny. He couldn't think of a time when any of the other brothers had been treated this way, either. So, it seemed the brotherhood was singling him out to test his responses. So be it.

"Why did you take it upon yourself to accelerate the timeline?"

Rex could feel the pressure behind the question. He was aware that by accelerating the baseline, many of the other targets in the overall plan would fall to the wayside. But the timing was secondary to the goal. In fact, the other points that would now be missed were of little importance to the overall goal. He interrupted his train of thought and stared back at Mr. Leon.   Now, he felt the unified connection of all of his brothers enter the back of his mind.   A sense of peace struck him, and he fell into the mental embrace of his family.

Mr. Leon smiled at the expression of contentment shining from Rex's face, "We needed to understand the reasons for your decision.   We also agree that the end goal outweighs all else, but we had to be sure."   Mr. Leon cocked his head to the side, "You have been... different... since your collapse aboard that freighter.   We hoped and prayed that you were still with us, still one of us.   And we are glad to know that you are."

Rex basked in the full connection with all of his brothers.   It was a rare moment amongst their own.

***

Rosa Keri was standing guard next to the door of the corporate office when a young man walked over and handed her a small package.   He said, "For your employer," as he gave a quick bow and backed away.   She watched him disappear around the corner, then she looked down quizzically at her palm.   The long, slim package she held had almost no weight.   The decorative paper that covered it was folded with the sharpest creases she had ever seen.

The door behind her opened and her boss strolled out past her.   He threw a wink her way and gestured for her to follow him. She double-stepped it over to catch up, then fell into his stride. She held the package out, but he just smiled and kept walking. With a roll of her eyes, she stuffed it under her arm to free up both of her hands.

"Where to now, oh Glorious Leader?" Rosa snidely asked.

Her employer extended his hand and indicated a small eatery hidden away in a dark corner at this end of the station. She headed toward it, but Rex Leon jumped ahead of her. He whisked out a chair and stood patiently behind it until she begrudgingly sat down. He slipped her chair under the small table before he plopped down into one himself. His hand motioned toward the gift-wrapped package. Rosa slid it toward him and began to ask, "Okay, Mr. Leon, what happ...?"

"First," Rex interrupted, "We are going to have a lovely cup of tea."

He delicately unwrapped the paper that encircled the small box with a glow of anticipation on his face. A foil package dropped free. He pulled out a tiny pair of scissors and carefully cut the bag open. An exquisite aroma wafted up from the small bag. An elderly gentleman brought over a steaming kettle and set it on the table, along with two cups and a tiny decorative clay pot. Then with a small bow, the man stepped away.

Rex Leon scooped out a spoonful of bright green rolled leaves and tipped them into the pot. He decanted hot water from the kettle over the leaves and covered them with the lid. Within a matter of seconds, the tea leaves brewed into a pale chartreuse liquid. He filled both cups, quickly laid claim to the one nearest himself, and settled back into his chair.

"I do hope you enjoy tea, Ms. Keri. It is difficult to find people these days with an interest in this very ancient practice."

Rosa picked up her cup and breathed in the steam. A fragrance both floral and grassy filled her nose. She took a sip and savored the flavor as she set the small cup back onto the table.

"At a guess, I'd say this batch came from one of the islands on Amemasu?" Rosa raised up the cup and breathed in the aroma again, "Mid growing season?" She tasted the tea once more. "Early to just the beginning of the mid growing season."

Rex flashed an astonished smile, "These leaves are originally from Amemasu! My, you are a treasure, Ms. Keri." He took a light swallow from his cup. "I will be quite honest. I did not expect someone with your history to know the finer nuances of tea. I mean no offense."

Rosa smirked as she placed her empty cup down on the table. "Well, when you grow up on a planet known for its tea leaves, you become quite aware of your competitors' products."

"Oh? You have picked tea? How exciting!" he crowed. "Which island?"

Rosa's mouth fell into a melancholy

smile, "Mr. Leon, I was born on the planet Makara in the Shukh system. My family owned a tea plantation in the mountainous region of Ketu, the largest inhabited island. When I was a child, Makaran tea was well known throughout a large portion of the Consortium, especially among the elite."

"Makaran tea? Yes, I've heard of it, but only in passing." His eyes closed as he cycled through his memories, "Isn't the stratosphere of Makara wracked with pollution?"

"It is now. It was pristine until fuel deposits were discovered under the oceans. The Consortium came with their contractors and began drilling. My people protested the mining when the side effects of it damaged the planet's waters." Sadness clouded Rosa's face, "As the waters became undrinkable, the plants died. Once the plants disappeared, the pollution blocked out the stars. My family was forced to sell the property to the corporations at a huge loss and barely covered some of the loans. We were left destitute. Eventually, my parents turned to the only work available on the planet... mining. And in a short time, that work took their lives."

The expression on Mr. Leon's face darkened. He poured more water into the pot and then tea into the two cups, "This saddens me."

"Me too," Rosa replied. "But thank you for this. I didn't think I would ever taste anything from my childhood again." She bowed her head in gratitude as she picked up the full cup and just held it in her hands, savoring her memories.

Mr. Leon watched as her eyes grew unfocused. He picked up his cup and took a sip. As the draught of tea hit the back of his throat, he joined her and stared off into the past.

twenty

The Bargain Store

The wormhole spun open and the Cyclops slipped out into the Ankara system. Once the yacht exited the jump gate ring, the automated systems completed the transaction for the travel charge. Anton sighed as their mazuma travel fund grew smaller. He threw a concerned glance at Barney, who sat at the comm. After a handful of minutes, the small man grunted and pulled off his headphones.

Barney caught Anton's look. "They must've gone to Baal Shamin," he grumbled. "I'm sure you know but we'll need bribes, a lot of bribes, just to make port."

Anton shifted over to the nav station and set the destination for the only planet in the system that had a visiting policy. Once the course was set, he unlocked the pilot's harness and gripped the comm station.

"We're running out of mazuma fast, Barney."

Barney pulled up the monetary records and rubbed his face, "If we don't hit a spot of luck, this search is going to become nigh impossible... and soon."

An entry in the financial records caught Anton's eyes. He shouldered Barney out of the way and rifled through the ledgers that had been recorded prior to their departure. He chuckled as he shunted one page over to the pilot's station, hopped over the console and slipped into the pilot's seat.

Barney curled his lip in irritation. He pulled up all the information he could glean about Baal Shamin. It was a small planet with a series of domed towns... cities would be too extravagant a word. Each one was owned by a rival company, though gang would be a more accurate term. He was going to have to stick to that comm channel as if life depended on it. Luli's life to be exact, he amended.

Anton shunted a screen back to the comm station, "Hey, Barney! Check this out!" He leapt over the console and landed next to his diminutive partner. Barney set aside his searches and opened the screen that Anton had sent over. His eyes grew big. He scrolled down through the screen and his eyes grew even larger.

"What did you do?" he asked.

Jon Gray Lang

"Where did this come from, Rabbit?" He glared at Anton, who beamed a smile in return. "Where did you get this?"

"Well, it seems that your home planet set up a floating bank account for these retrieval ships," Anton explained. "So, I, uh... made a withdrawal."

Barney's face darkened considerably at this news.

"It's not like that, Barney. I went through the account history. The withdrawals were taken in large sums, but in a relatively rhythmic pattern."

Barney's eyes burned into him.

"Don't give me that look," he blurted. "It was about time for another withdrawal to occur! We want it to look like the Titan retrieval team is still operating, right? I figure this is one of the ways they track their dealings." His voice grew quiet as he studied Barney, "I'm doing this to keep you safe."

"And we need the mazuma," Barney grunted. "We're leaving another digital trail out there. Let's hope no one is looking for it. Well, except for the ones we want to see it."

The comm erupted with chatter. Barney grabbed the headphones and squelched the signals until he found the voice from the Demetrius again. With a little more finessing, the comm came in much cleaner now. His grin reflected on the console as he scrawled a location down and shunted it over to the nav station.

"Good news. We have a destination."

***

"I hope this gift conveys our desire to visit your fine city," said Anton.

"It is a handsome gift," replied the latest contact through the ship's comm. "Make your way to our fine city, and please, enjoy your stay in the jewel of Baal Shamin."

"We look forward to seeing the wondrous sights of Tellerium. Cyclops out." Anton clicked the comm off and watched their finances take another hit. "I guess I should be happy it only took fives contacts to gain access, but it hurts to watch our mazuma drop so quickly."

"Stolen mazuma," Barney quipped as he maneuvered the Cyclops into berth slot F-0.451. "Help me with the lockdown procedures."

"On it," replied Anton as the port map dumped to the Cyclops computer. "Seriously? The port is nowhere near Tellerium. Can this trip get any more expensive?"

Barney flicked the main switch and the hum from the ship's life support faded away. "We're on their air now. Hopefully, the amount you withdrew will cover the cost."

Anton shrugged as he raided the yacht's safe, "Knock on plasteel."

Barney grumbled as he shrugged into the Titan's priest robes. He brushed at the front of the vestments until it flattened and his hands dropped to rest aggressively on his hips.

"You look stunningly official," mocked Rabbit.

"Shut it..."

Their funds took another hit at the Port of Call desk. Thankfully, it was a fruitful endeavor when they walked away with the Demetrius' berthing slot. The individual behind the desk had also mentioned that three men were seen leaving the vessel and heading to the city. Barney stepped off to the side and motioned to Anton toward a corner out of earshot of the desk.

"Want me to check out the Demetrius?" Anton whispered.

Barney was quiet in response. Then he pulled Anton closer, "I think you should follow them into town. My size and this stupid outfit will make me conspicuous. I have a better chance of not drawing attention if I stay here close to the ship."

"I don't know," Anton said. "I think that might be dangerous."

Barney shoved him away and grinned darkly, "You are in my employ, Mr. Roane. Do as I command, or I will find someone who will!" Barney defiantly marched deeper into the port.

"Well, I guess that settles it then," Anton muttered under his breath as he watched Barney walk away.

***

Jon Gray Lang

With furtive glances, Barney made his way back to the Cyclops. Once the hallway emptied around him, he stripped off the priest garments and unceremoniously dropped them onto the floor. He nudged it into a dark corner, and cursed, "Dreadful rag! I have more important things to do than play dress up."

Barney quickly made his way back to the main hub. It didn't take long to find the correct wing for the Demetrius. "Pretty damn empty out here. Wonder if they paid extra to keep people out of their business."

Berth number T-1.138 blinked haphazardly above a single hatch at the end of the corridor, "This is the place."

Barney stole a peek over his shoulder as he pulled the panel cover off the tunnel lock. He connected a couple of wires from his data pad to the exposed electronics and fiddled with the screen. With a loud click, the hatch door slid open. Barney quickly unhooked his data pad and rehung the panel cover.

He shuffled into the tunnel. The hatch closed behind him with another loud click. He stepped gingerly down the shaft with all of his senses on high alert. All the information indicated the Demetrius was empty, except for the deep spacer they were tailing.

Barney checked his vest pockets. "What did Luli used to say? The best way to prepare for everything is to be unprepared... or some such nonsense."

Preoccupied with that thought, he almost walked headfirst into the ship's hatch. Corrosion pitted the corners of the hatch lock cover and filthy grease leaked from underneath. It was wedged in pretty tight, but with a bit of swearing, Barney pried it loose. Once the cover was off, he just stared at the inner workings.

"How bloody old is this thing?" he groused. "I've only ever seen one of these in a manual and that was ages ago!"

The apparatus was ancient and completely mechanical. He spied a crank bar hidden in a notch and a giant gear with a keyed hole in its center. He grabbed the crank bar and jammed it into the hole. By the time he'd made a gap in the hatch just big enough for him to squeak through, sweat soaked his shirt collar. He hastily jammed the crank bar back into its notch and squeezed through the gap. Closing the hatch required another sweat intensive effort, but at least he was inside.

***

On his own now, Anton glanced up at the directional signs and followed the green arrow to the subway system. The port for Tellerium resembled a half circle where the corridors to the berth slots branched outward. The main hub was centrally located and ran inward under the ground to the subway system.

"Make way!" a guard shouted as she forced Anton to the side. A long line of people followed her through a door marked 'Authorized Personnel Only'. It took a moment for him to realize they had been chained together. He shook his head in disbelief as he continued walking toward the subway.

When Baal Shamin had first been colonized, the corrosive nature of the atmosphere had forced the people to build underground. Over time, the size of the colony had grown, and domes had been built along the surface. The outer skin of the domes was treated with a special coating that slowed down the deterioration from the atmosphere, but even that had to be replaced once a planetary year. This thankless job fell to the poorest inhabitants of this rock as well as to those in debtors prison.

The Arrival/Departure sign in the subway station showed that a train was due in three minutes. The next one would not arrive for another half hour. As Anton moved quickly across the crowded platform, he noticed three brutish men that looked very familiar. What were the odds that the very people he was searching for would be standing only a few shoulder widths away? Luck was on his side.

The train rattled down the tracks and came to a rough stop. A chime sounded and the sliding doors parted open. Two of the men struggled to get a large duffle bag into one of the cars. Once they were aboard, Anton followed them in and slouched against the wall.

The train jerked to a start, then suddenly picked up momentum and shot toward the city. The lights flickered with each jarring motion, but the speed wasn't affected. After fifteen minutes of being on his feet, Anton wished he had grabbed a seat. His knees ached thanks to the short pilot seat on the Cyclops. Focusing on his discomfort kept his mind occupied for the rest of the journey.

It came as a surprise when the brakes screeched at last, and the car shook from the deceleration. The train ground to a halt and the hiss of pressurized gases being released reverberated through the car. Anton quickly pushed away from the wall and slipped off the train. He searched for a vantage point to watch the people who exited the train.

Soon he spotted two of the men as they muscled their way through the sliding doors with the duffle bag. They didn't seem to care about what was in the bag as it was banged against everything before it finally cleared the doors. They joined the third man and spoke to him in hushed tones. Anton strained to hear what they said, but there was just too much noise in the station.

The three men exchanged nods, then one of them joined the foot traffic off to the right. The other two shifted their grip on the bag and headed through the left exit.

"Damn it!" Anton cursed. "What do I do? Follow the loner or go after the two bag men?"

***

If the Demetrius had seen better days, Barney assumed it must have been way before his time. Filth seemed to bleed out of the bulkheads. Trash and detritus lay in the corners of the airlock that was just as grimy as the main throughway of the ship. The cramped cockpit was stacked with empty food and drink containers. The whole ship stank of gear oil that hadn't been changed in a lifetime and unwashed human bodies. Doorways branched off the throughway that continued toward the rear of the ship.

In the first cabin, a strange assortment of knickknacks littered the floor. One, in particular, grabbed his attention. A random beam of light reflected off of the helmet attached by a spring to a heavily worn figurine wearing an old Earth spacesuit. In size it was not much bigger than a standard data pad. For some reason the piece called to him, so he crammed it into one of his many pockets.

He couldn't shake the feeling that something was watching him as he stepped into the second cabin. "Quit looking for ghosts, Barney," he rebuked himself. "This relic is empty."

A small pile of synthetic scalps

stacked on an end table caught his eye, "Gods! Sick, twisted bastards. One of these better not be Luli's."

Once he left the living quarters of the ship, the design of the bulkheads changed. The next section was crammed with all manner of equipment. Some of it was recognizable as radio equipment and the like. He didn't have a clue what some of it was for. Past this section hung an enormous bundle of holding tanks. He ran his hand along one of them, "Must be fuel canisters or some other holdover from its colonial days."

He spied an oddly-shaped hatch that was partially obscured by the comm station. He pressed his ear against the metal, and noted it was deathly quiet on the other side. As delicately as he could, he grasped the handle on the hatch and gave it a slow push. The click of it unlatching echoed amongst the tanks in the back room. Barney froze in place. Nothing strange happened, so he edged into the opening for a peek in. But the room was pitch black.

Barney flipped the light switch on the inner wall. The lights guttered and buzzed and a sickly greenish hue permeated the room. "What in all nine hells..." The walls were haphazardly sprayed with lubricant and blood. Ribbons of synthetic flesh lay in piles along the floor. Something about all of it was recognizable, like a pattern he had seen before, "The prison ship we rescued Rabbit from..."

The room was set up like a shrine for slaughter. A metal bowl crusted in dried blood sat in the center of what could only be some sort of altar. Hastily painted black lettering in a language that Barney didn't recognize decorated the pedestal of the altar. And barely visible inside the bowl was a curious cylinder.

Barney walked over and had to stand on his toes to reach the object. He pulled out the bloodied cylinder and turned it over and over in his hands. It took him a moment to realize what it was; a memory core.

"Please don't let this be Luli's," he implored.

***

Anton grimaced, "Luli better not be in that duffle bag, but there's only one way to find out."

He hung back as far as was possible while still keeping them in sight. However, this was becoming more difficult by the minute. The hallways they traveled down were growing sparse of pedestrians. At some point, Anton would easily be seen.

Luckily, the two men ahead of him still seemed oblivious to his presence as he followed them. They headed down into the industrial section of the underground city. This was where the air converters, water pumps and all the other needed accoutrements for life on an unlivable world existed. Unfortunately, they had passed only a couple of other people in the past twenty minutes and Anton was getting nervous.

The two men stopped, so Anton quickly slipped into a dark crevice that offered a limited view ahead. He couldn't quite make out what they were doing, but a rusty hinge squeaked, followed by a loud clang. Anton tried moving to a better position but knocked over an empty bottle in his haste.

***

"What was that?" asked the larger of the two men.

The other one grabbed both ends of the bag and motioned with his shoulder, "Go check it out, Marcus."

Marcus nodded as he pulled a well-used pistol from the inside of his coat, "On it."

He moved gingerly toward where the noise originated, and his eyes pierced the shadows. He tracked along the dripping pipes that ran down the walls until he spotted the toe of a shoe sticking out. He poked his head into the crevice, but it was dark. With a grimace, he holstered the pistol and pulled out a small cylinder. He played the beam of light from the pocket flash into the shadows.

With a low chuckle, he shook his head and put away the flash. He relaxed as he strolled back to help with the bag. It took some effort, but they eventually got the bag to fall into the dumpster.

"What was it?" The larger man asked as he let the dumpster lid crash down.

Marcus finished folding the now-empty duffle bag and shoved it under his arm. "It was nothing, Franco. Just some drunk sleeping it off. You want me to get rid of him?"

"Naw, no need," Franco shrugged as he walked back the way they had come. "We're getting off this rock pretty soon."

"Not even for a little fun?" wheedled Marcus.

Franco laughed as he smacked him on the shoulder, "Get on you. Plenty of time for that later."

***

Anton kept his eyes closed until the voices disappeared into the distance. It had been a long time since he had slept one off out in the streets, but at the moment, he was glad for the experience. The best way to make an act believable was with experience.

He edged out into the hallway slowly and made sure no one else was out there. Nothing moved toward him when he stood up and dusted himself off. He sighed at a prominent stain that now colored his jacket and decided he didn't want to know what it was. With all the stealth he could muster, he carefully approached the dumpster.

He opened the lid quietly and peeked

in. The light was poor, so he popped out his flash and shown it inside. The marred and lifeless face of the missing Yannick Specht stared back at him.

"At least it's not Luli..." Anton breathed in relief.

As he closed the lid, his elation at this revelation made him feel worse for the poor man inside the dumpster. But he was glad to know he and Barney were following the right people. And if they hadn't dumped Luli on some other planet, there was a good chance they might find her soon.

Anton listened intently as he wiped his hands against his now soiled pant leg, but he didn't hear anyone. Certain that he was alone, he decided to run all the way back. The hallways echoed with the sound of his feet slapping the ground until he emerged into the main thoroughfare. Sweat glistened along his brow as he scanned the crowd for the killers, but they were nowhere to be seen.

Anton bolted further into town but still didn't catch sight of them anywhere. He stopped to catch his breath. His mind cycled through what information he did have. Three men had come to this planet to dump a body. Surely, they would want to get off-planet quickly.

His eyes widened at the thought. With a quick turn, he ran back to the train station. There was a good chance he might catch them on their way back to the Demetrius. He pushed his way through the crowd at the gate to the subway. He stood up on his toes, just in time to see all three culprits board a subway car.

Anton shoved his way through the line ignoring the dark looks and comments that rewarded his efforts. By the time he cleared the tangle of the crowd, he could only stare in dismay as the subway train rolled away from the station and down the line to the ship port. With a quick glance up to the Arrival/Departure sign, he saw that the next train was a half-hour away.

"Shit!" he swore as he smacked his fist against his leg.

***

Shaken, Barney stumbled out of the torture room. Feeling weak, he braced himself against the lowest of the tanks in the backroom. When a sudden noise startled him, he hunkered down in a dark corner. Two bruisers entered the equipment section. They walked into a small room Barney hadn't noticed on his way through the ship. As they both reappeared laughing, their conversation drifted toward him. The shorter of the two men stopped next to the radio equipment, while the other walked past Barney's hiding place. Barney heard a series of switches click and saw the fuel monitors flare on each of the tanks and glow eerily in the half-light.

"I swear we need to get this bloody radio wired into the cockpit," swore the heavy-set man near the radio equipment. "It's ridiculous having to come way back here to get all our comms done."

"You just don't want to walk, Ian," the other man mocked.

"C'mon Franco, you know that the gravity back here is stronger," Ian lamented. "It kills my back. I'm not as young as I used to be."

"You're not as fit either."

An overhead comm kicked on, "Where are we, guys? Are we ready to go?"

"Everything at this end is ready," stated Franco.

Ian grumbled a moment before he replied, "Calling the port tower now. I'll meet you both up there in a few minutes."

Franco strolled past the radio equipment, "Say something sweet to Orisa if she's working the comm. Would you?"

"Sure, sure," Ian muttered as he keyed the comm, "Demetrius to Port Control. Demetrius to Port Control, please come in."

"Port Control to Demetrius, this is Port Control."

"Orisa, is that you?"

"Yes. Is that you, Ian?"

"Sure is. Franco wanted to give you some sugar."

Laughter erupted over the comm, "I keep telling him, I'm a married woman."

"Listening was never his strong point.

We're looking for clearance to leave. Think you can speed that up for us?"

"Sure thing, honey" Orisa answered. "It's a slow day. You're up in the next thirty minutes."

"Thanks, Orisa. Ian, I mean Demetrius out."

"Roger, Demetrius. You tell Franco that my husband has been ill for the past few days. If you guys stayed in port a little longer..."

Ian laughed, "I'll let him know Orisa, but you shouldn't play with him like that. He'll never learn!"

Laughter rang out over the comm as Ian cut the link and shut the board down. He wandered off in the direction of the cockpit.

Barney stayed hidden in the back room until he was sure they weren't returning. He cursed, "Now I'm stuck on this piece of junk! What am I going to do?"

twenty-one

Mothership Connection (Star Child)

Anton paced persistently as the train's half-empty car sped it's way back to the port hub. Those bastards were half an hour ahead. So much could happen in that span of time. He had tried to contact Barney, but this planet's crust hampered the signal, adding to his frustration.

With a screech of the brakes, the car rattled and Anton held tighter to the pole beside the exit doors. If the Demetrius had taken off, then all his efforts were for naught. He had to get ahold of Barney. The train slowly rolled to a stop and the doors opened. Anton hopped out and ran for the exit gate. He made a beeline for the port desk and slapped the counter loudly to get the attention of the attendant.

A heavily lidded woman with the name Orisa stenciled across her badge ambled over and gave him an appraising look. Her fingers tapped furiously against her screen as she drawled, "Mr. Roane?"

Anton nodded, "Wait, how do you know my name?"

Her left eyebrow slowly arched.

He stammered, "Has the Demetrius left port yet?"

"We don't share the comings and goings of rival merchants, sir."

Anton slid a few bills over to her. She just stared at him until he rummaged around in his pockets and added a few more to the wrinkled heap.

Her attitude brightened considerably, "The answer is no. But they are set to leave in the next ten minutes."

"Damn it!" He slapped at the countertop and pushed himself away. As he took off running to the berth slot for the Cyclops, he shouted over his shoulder, "Thanks for the information!"

"Hey!" cried a crewman as Anton shouldered past him.

Anton kept running and Barney sprung to his mind. Maybe he could get ahead of their departure.

He switched on the personal comm,

"Barney, you copy? Barney, you there?"

His voice echoed back at him from the passageway ahead. Uncertainty struck him as he slowed down to look for the cause. He muttered back into the comm, "Barney?"

" ...Barney?" echoed faintly from a dimly lit corner of the wall.

He reached down and his fingers snagged on a piece of cloth. With a light tug, the whole length of the priest robe flopped out and a personal comm unit clattered to the floor. With fear eating at his heart, he looked both ways down the tunnel, then picked up the comm unit.

"Where the hell are you, Barney?"

***

Rex Leon stepped into the boarding tunnel leading to the Independence and was quickly followed by Rosa. The story of her bleak childhood had altered his opinion of her and changed his expectations. She had been stranded on her home world with little direction, yet she had ventured out into the wild universe alone to try to make a difference. Unfortunately, she had fallen in with the wrong crowd and was stuck once again. The regret she carried regarding past decisions weighed heavily upon her. In some ways, that made him trust her all the more.

The walk through the tube to the ship was quiet, but the air was unusually brisk. He wrapped his arms around himself to ease the chill. A small puff of dust popped against the tunnel wall near his shoulder, followed quickly by another. Then two more resounding pops echoed back from the far end of the shaft. Rosa shoved him hard from behind and Rex stumbled forward.

"Go!" she screamed at him as she ripped out a pistol from under her jacket.

He didn't bother second-guessing what she said, and ran full tilt toward the Independence. There was that ironic name again, he smiled, like some kind of ongoing joke. A loud report behind him was followed shortly by a sudden scream. He glanced back to see Rosa Keri straddling one man on the walkway of the tunnel while she was being attacked by three other assailants. Further down the tunnel, he saw another kill squad running toward her.

He quickened his pace and pounded on the airlock hatch. As the hatch cycled open another shot pinged against the airlock wall. He cried out as he stumbled into the hangar bay, "Delta! Delta! Get your people down there now!"

Three soldiers bolted past him armed with heavy assault rifles. Their shots punctured the lining of the tunnel and the atmosphere began to bleed out.

He watched Rosa fall to her knees clutching her side, "Damn it all, where is my sword?"

He turned and ran back down the tunnel, just as Rosa fell face-first to the decking. Her pistol slipped from her hand and skittered against the tunnel wall. She looked pale and her jacket was soaked with her blood. He dropped to his knees, grabbed her fallen pistol and fired it into the crowd gathered at the station end of the tunnel. Soldiers who had taken up positions near Rosa, bolted forward and fired repeatedly into the mob.

The remainder of the crowd retreated, then dispersed back into the station leaving their dead behind. Two genorgs took up positions against the station's airlock while a third one cycled it closed. Once it was locked, they sprinted back toward the ship. Rex looked down at Rosa and her eyes fluttered open.

"It's good to see you're still breathing, Rosa," he declared. "We will have need of your skills very soon, I presume."

Two of the genorgs stopped and looked questioningly at Mr. Leon. When he waved toward Rosa, they slung their rifles and bent down to pick her up. The motors that controlled the tunnel retraction rumbled to life and it began to pull in and collapse. Mr. Leon stood up quickly and a wave of dizziness hit him. The air in the tunnel was already lower than was safe.

"We'll need to hurry this up, ladies," Mr. Leon stared at the airlock hatch on the station, "Or this is going to end badly."

"I... I saved the tea," Rosa spoke weakly. "I may have bled on it, though."

"Oh, Commander Keri," Rex smiled

down at her as she fumbled the package out from the inside of her jacket pocket, "You are a woman of wonders. Far beyond what I expected. I am so very glad you accepted my offer of employment."

***

Jacquie wiped the sweat from her brow. The struggle to get Galena's limp body into the med tube had been difficult, especially since Doc had refused to help.

"You'll look after her, right?" she asked.

It had taken some powerful convincing, but Doc finally had agreed that he would repair Galena. When Jacquie left the sickbay, she heard the automaton squawk that the Lieutenant was a waste of resources.

Jacquie had uncoupled the Matilda from the station, but without a destination, she didn't know where to set course. For the time being, she simply set the trajectory for the jump gate, while she watched ship after ship leave the station all bound for that same objective. The mass exodus she witnessed meant there wouldn't be a single freighter left on the station... and that would be a rare occurrence. A complete lack of space-bound traffic could reduce a station down to financial ruin.

Space stations depended on the flow of goods and currency to stay in business. And just like any other kind of trading post, if that flow trickled down to a stop, it died. Never mind that this station had been robbed blind and from what Galena had told her, there wasn't a genorg miner left to work on the planet. The whole colony would be dead unless the Consortium did something drastic.

"It's been a long time, Jacq," said a male voice close behind her.

With a gasp, she spun around and drew her pistol in a single fluid motion. The man she'd recently fished out from under the comm station stood before her. His arms raised in quick surrender as he backed away.

"Whoa! Hey there, Captain... let's take it easy."

In disgust, Jacquie slammed her pistol back into its holster and crossed her arms, "Hau Hung..."

A smirk skittered across his face, "Very well, thank you."

She groaned in exasperation, "You and that damn joke. I had hoped to never hear it again."

Hung quirked an eyebrow, "It's good to see you again, too. And I must say, you're looking pretty fine."

"Stop," she snarled. "Don't do that. You had your chance years ago and you blew it."

"My, my. So touchy." He backed up and glanced down the hallway, "Where's the incomparable Luli Qing? I haven't seen that babe in a long time. They don't make them like they used to

Jon Gray Lang

and I could do with a... reunion."

A multitude of mixed emotions wrestled across Jacquie's face, "She's not here."

Mr. Hau abandoned his leer and assumed a poker face, "So, the rumors are true then."

"I was told that you would be giving me a destination for all those crates in my hold," growled Jacquie. "I need to be long gone from this place before the Consortium figures out it's been gutted."

The boorish man plopped himself down at the nav station and keyed up a star chart, "Yes, right. I'd prefer not to meet up with them, either. Something about a misunderstanding on their part, you know."

"I'm sure it was," Jacquie agreed as she slid into the pilot's seat. She pulled up the star chart in the visor and blinked at it, "Baal Shamin? What could anyone possibly need in that shithole?"

"None of your concern at the moment," he replied. "But that's where you need to take the cargo. Got it?"

A light blinked at the comm station as mail from the jump gate was dumped to the Matilda. Hau Hung sidled over and toggled off the light before she noticed it.

"Alright then. Be your usual sneaky underhanded self." She glared at him and motioned to the comm station, "Since you're over there, why don't you make yourself useful and get permission from the jump gate tower? I have to prep Matilda for this." Her face locked into the visor.

Hung's mouth curled into a devilish smile as he went through the new mail. One of them had been about a genorg uprising on a factory planet. Another had been about a strike on some station in one a system on the edge of nowhere. The last one was a report of a locked jump gate at an outlying system. He deleted each one. He searched for the message he had been told to watch for, from a ship called the Cyclops. When the icon for it disappeared, he keyed the comm to the jump gate and requested a travel permit to the Ankara system.

"We're on our way, Captain Delahaye."

***

The Waratah passed through the jump gate and entered the Ankara system. No new messages from either the Cyclops or the Matilda came through, so Derain set course for Baal Shamin. He hoped this meant he might at least catch up with Barney and Rabbit. After the loss of his family on Aketi, he could use the company.

It would also be a relief to get out of this spacesuit and breathe someone else's canned air. Maybe take a shower, too, or at least have a moment to recollect. The ship's sensor alarm began to blink rapidly and he toggled it off. It registered a transponder that was pretty far away, but it was traveling in his direction.

Something familiar about the transponder code snagged his attention. He ran it through the Waratah's database, and it pinged back a response. The code belonged to a vessel called the Demetrius.

He let the name cycle through his mind. Then it hit him, "That's the ship the Cyclops was chasing! Maybe they aren't down on the planet after all," he mused. "Maybe they had a run with the crew of the Demetrius and lost."

He pulled the schematic Mr. Leon had given him. The target craft was large, much larger than the Cyclops or the Waratah. It was almost twice as long as the Matilda, but its storage capacity was minuscule in comparison.

With a few taps to the attitude jets, his trajectory altered to a course that should take him in close to her flight path. He shut down most of the ship's systems and ran dark.

After a couple of hours, the temperature of his ship had dropped enough that it would barely register on a random sweep. By the time he could actually see the Demetrius, he calculated, the Waratah should show up as a chunk of space trash. He watched as it grew closer and shivered slightly with excitement. But the Demetrius didn't ping his boat or even change direction. It continued to move inexorably outward.

Derain muttered aloud, "Where are

they going?"

He poured over his star charts for this system, but there were no planets, moons or stations along the course the Demetrius had chosen. The ship's path would take it farther away from the jump gate and civilization. It made no sense.

The Demetrius spun slowly as it grew larger in his port bow. A series of long tubes ran from the midsection to the bow only to coalesce into a large boxlike container located just under the nose. Derain stared at it quizzically, trying to guess its purpose, when a peculiar light suddenly materialized at the end of the construct. His expression changed from confusion to understanding.

He cursed into his helmet, "No. No. No! No!"

The very edge of a wormhole appeared out past the bow port. While the Demetrius slipped past his dropship, he watched in utter hopelessness as the wormhole continued to grow wider. The long spacecraft elongated into the wormhole before it rubber-banded back into shape and disappeared through the eye. The wormhole shrank in size until it disintegrated in front of the Waratah.

"A wormhole drive? Where did they get a wormhole drive? No one's allowed to own a wormhole drive!"

Derain glared in frustration at the empty sector of space where, as far as he knew, the only lead to Luli had just disappeared. Did Barney or Anton have something that would help? Was the Matilda on its way here? Were any of his friends even alive still? His hands clenched into fists as he considered his options.

There were no answers out there. His only hope was to see if any lay on the planet. If nothing else, he could find out if the Cyclops had actually made it to the surface or not. With precise movements that were a little too forceful, he keyed in a route to Baal Shamin.

At least it was somewhere to go.

twenty-two

Good Old Girl

The cabin was illuminated by dim pinpricks of light shining from the ship's comm, and Galena welcomed that. Her head flopped against a pillow as she awaited the arrival of sleep, but her eyes were still open, scanning the darkness around her. Uncertainty tinged her thoughts, "*Is this reality? ...or am I in a dream?*"

She felt like a fragment... a tiny particle of a much larger organism. An organism that was comprised of millions of separate pieces. Yet each tiny piece was acutely aware that it was also part of one large, singular, totally complete organism. Like the notes of a song.

Too many visions circled through her head, so jumbled together that Galena couldn't fully concentrate on any one of them. Some images seemed familiar.   Others were otherworldly, horrifying or surreal to her.   Her nerve endings tingled with a million sensations.   Her body struggled with the feeling of falling, of submersion, of being crushed all at the same time.   Floating to the weightless edge of sleep, then jerked into consciousness, her mind fought its way back to reality where two questions lingered: Who was she? And shouldn't she know?

"I... I am Galena..." the words stuttered faintly from her lips, reverberating with thousands of phantom voices that repeated her statement like a mantra.   It seemed that just her name itself provided the only anchor in the sea of her bewilderment. Her hand sought for the dog tags encircling her neck and she tried again, "I am Galena... Galena Chadov..."

She fought to close her ears to the echoes bouncing through her skull.   She willed herself to separate from them. She wasn't sure who or what they were.

"Are they me?" she asked.

The voices repeated her question, "Are they me? Are they me? Are they me? Are we her? Are we one? Are we one?"

***

Galena's eyes snapped open, but she couldn't see. She began to hyperventilate and her hands slapped against the sides of the med tube.

Jon Gray Lang

She reached for the latch and the lid softly popped as it opened.

She sat up and looked around the sickbay. Her blurry vision cleared just enough for her to discern Doc sliding on his track toward her. She jerked back in surprise when he slammed to a stop right next to her tube.

"Sho sho du ka te no!" Doc's voice barked. "Sho che ta me klo."

She squinted under the bright lights Doc used as he examined her. And she definitely had the feeling that the noises he made as he slid away were insults directed at her.

She groaned as she grasped the edge of the med tube and hoisted herself out. As soon as her feet touched the ground, her head erupted with a pounding. She reached up to rub it and discovered her head was wrapped tightly in gauze. Her fingers felt along her scalp and found that the pain centered close to her left temple.

"What happened?" she asked the empty air.

She moved toward Doc, but he whisked away from her and continued to curse her.

"Fine!" she cried out.

She shuffled out into the cargo bay and onto the lift. Within seconds, the doors parted, and she headed to the bridge. Her skull felt like it was too tight against the skin. She grew faint and clutched at the hatch to keep from falling in. When the rolling pain subsided, she stepped onto the bridge.

Through the bow port she could see the inside of a wormhole. The end of the portal was approaching quickly. The Matilda shuddered as it broke through and flew past the jump gate. Galena held on to the hatch as she was jostled about by the sudden turbulence.

"Where are we going?" she asked aloud.

***

At the sound of the Lieutenant's voice, Jacquie's head popped out of the visor and her hand went for her pistol. Adrenaline rushed through her at the memory of their last encounter. But she realized the Lieutenant's eyes were clear now, so she slid her hand away from the pistol and forced herself to relax.

"We've just entered the Ankara system, as per our cargo's instructions." Wary concern clouded Jacquie's face, "How are you feeling?"

Mr. Hau interjected, "I could tell you how she's feeling."

Galena punched Hung in the gut, then clutched at her head, "Augh! It feels like someone just drove an armor-piercing round into my brain."

Jacquie relaxed even more watching

Galena strike Hung. She seemed more like her old self, but best to be cautious. If Doc hadn't been there, who knows how things would've turned out?

The Lieutenant eased into the seat at the weapons station, "So the human speaks useful words. What's the natural-born's name?"

"His name is Hau Hung," he answered before Jacquie could. "And the answer is always, quite well, thank you."

"By the Major! You and that tiresome joke! Can't you just leave it alone for once?" Jacquie got up and examined Galena's bandage, "You took a nasty hit to the head."

"I figured that much. Now if only I had a clue what happened."

Jacquie leaned in close and whispered, "You had a... a seizure and you hurt yourself."

Galena nodded but her eyes shimmered with fear, "Do we have a destination in this system?"

Hau Hung blithely relayed, "We're heading to Baal Shamin and all of it's corporate fiefdom. You two will need to do a pickup. Since this job will need both of you, it is good to see you up."

"Why both of us?" asked Jacquie.

Mr. Hau replied, "The people who have the package won't exactly be willing to part with it."

"We're not thieves, Hung. Why do you think we would we do this?"

A predacious smile punctuated his response, "Let's be honest, Jacq. Some of your crew steal. Some are murderers, and you bootleg contraband. Every last one of you are thieves of some sort."

Anger blistered across Jacquie's face. Hung instinctively threw up his hands to calm her, "Two points really. First, you didn't ask the right questions and you already took the job. Secondly, the word is you're looking for someone. My contact who set this whole operation in motion may have a lead on your pilot."

***

The flight hours of this trip had dragged on endlessly and Derain was grateful to finally make his approach to Baal Shamin. He paid the exorbitant kickback and slid the Waratah into berth slot E-1.701. With a sense of urgency, he locked the dropship up and headed off toward the port desk.

"I don't mind saying, but it feels good to be out of that spacesuit."

It had become tiresome having to wear it whenever he traveled on the Waratah. He scowled at the idea of missing the comforts of the Matilda, but, in truth, he really did.

He muttered under his breath, "Who knows where she is. Who knows where any of us are?"

Jon Gray Lang

Derain decided to bypass the port desk and headed into the town proper for some food and a room. After the past few days of riding in a vacuum, this planet's gravity made his back ache. Maybe a hot shower, too. He pulled out the mazuma he had left in his hand and reconsidered his options.

"Looks like a cheap meal and maybe a bed instead," he grimaced. "If I'm lucky."

The train ride into town was quiet. It was late enough that most of the travelers had already found their way to the bars and eateries scattered under this dome. Based purely on its location, Derain headed toward a remote saloon located in the poor district.

The place was packed, but a waiter found a table for him near the kitchen. It was a tiny thing on three legs, however, since he was alone, it would do. The menu featured some delicious sounding entrees... none of which he could afford. With regret, he ordered the cheapest thing they had, heated protein solids.

The dish looked as appetizing as it sounded. An aroma similar to a loaf of bread and refried beans wafted up from his plate. He had eaten worse things in his life. As he chewed on the meal, suddenly the hairs on the back of his neck prickled. Someone was watching him. He ignored the sensation, until it became too distracting.

His eyes darted around the room searching for the culprit when suddenly a very familiar and surprisingly welcome voice exclaimed, "Derain? Is that really you?"

"Rabbit?"

Anton practically leapt over the table to face him. He grabbed a chair from a nearby table and slid into it. A big grin split his face as he looked Derain up and down, "Man, is it good to see you! I wasn't sure if you got our message."

Derain smiled back, "It's really good to see you too."

"What the hell are you eating?" Anton asked disdainfully. He grabbed the plate and threw it into the nearest waste bin.

Derain blurted, "That's my dinner! What are you doing?"

Anton ignored him and flagged down a waiter. He aggressively pointed at Derain, "Put him on my tab. Come with me, Mr. Tiwi."

Derain followed him to a larger table and sat down as he was told. The waiter walked over to the new table, but before he could say a word, Anton ordered, "He'll have the house special. And would you be so kind as to make us a couple of your favorite cocktails?" He winked and handed the waiter a small bundle of mazuma.

The waiter looked befuddled, but his face brightened when he counted out the mazuma in his hands.

Feeling a bit flustered, Derain sat quietly as a plate of luscious looking food was placed in front of him, along with a very tall drink.

It looked as if a bouquet of wildflowers had sprouted from the top of the glass, and the liquid inside gave off its own glow.

"What did you...? How did you...?" Derain stumbled through sentences.

"Here! Cheers to running into each other!" Anton shouted and clinked his glass against Derain's.

Derain shrugged and took a sip. "What is in this?"

"Not important right now," Anton grinned as he set down his glass. "Now, I'm only assuming you got our message. How did your search fare?"

Derain began, "Well, I..."

Anton interrupted him, "We'll get to that later. Here's how things stand right now." He leaned in close and whispered into Derain's ear, "We found Yannick, or what was left of him, after we tracked him to the Demetrius."

"So, we know who killed them. Good," Derain replied. "Now we just need to know where they're going."

Anton took a sip from his drink, "Exactly. But I lost them here. They took off and the Port Authority wouldn't let me leave in time to follow them. There must be some massive shipments leaving because, I can't get another travel permit until tomorrow night." The frustration was evident in his voice, "By then, they'll be long gone!"

Derain finished a bite of his dinner

and set down his fork, "You wouldn't have been able to follow them anyway. The Demetrius has a wormhole generator. I watched the ship disappear just after I cleared the jump gate."

The hope in Anton's face dissolved into discouragement.

Derain swallowed another bite, "Where's Barney? Is he here with you?"

Anton took a swig of his drink as he waved down the waiter and ordered two more. "No, he's not here. Best I can figure is Barney is on that ship."

"Damn it," cursed Derain. "I swear at every turn its one step forward and two steps back."

Anton's data pad trilled briefly and he retrieved it from a pocket. His eyebrows shot up for a moment before he stuffed the unit back into his coat. "We might have a bit of luck after all. A feeler I threw out earlier has reeled us into a meeting tomorrow. Fingers crossed it's another step forward."

"Fingers crossed," replied Derain as he took a healthy quaff from his drink. "Now if only I could get a hot shower."

"I can help with that," offered Anton.

***

Anton yawned and stretched as he got out of bed. He stared at the door to the toilet and heard the water running. Steam escaped under the door crack and he checked his data pad. Time was passing quickly.

"Derain! You done in the shower?" Anton pounded at the door. "C'mon man, we have got to go! Time's a'wastin'!"

***

Galena squinted and shaded her eyes, "Why is it so bright down here?"

"Doesn't seem that bright to me," answered Hung.

Jacquie growled, "Come one, let's get this over with."

She kept her eye on Galena all the way down to the cargo bay. She seemed normal, but it was obvious that the amount of pain she was in had increased. It didn't help that Doc had given Galena a troubling diagnosis. Not only was the Lieutenant's brain concussed, but the chip inside her skull now had a short. From what Barney had said, that chip was all that kept the alien mutagen in check. Doc didn't know what to do except prescribe enforced bed rest. And that wasn't possible right now.

Jacquie sighed as she stepped off the lift and followed her companions to the airlock. Doc didn't believe Galena's concussion was life-threatening, just that it would become more painful and the automaton was fine with that. For this job, Doc had injected her full of mood modifiers, muscle relaxers, and pain killers in the hope that it would ease her discomfort.

She muttered under breath, "Let's hope she can keep it together long enough to get us through this."

Jacquie locked down the Matilda and stepped out onto docking slot S-8.472 of Baal Shamin. This port had the same industrial appearance that most planet-bound docks shared. She gazed at the scenery and quickened her pace. Eventually, Jacquie caught up with Hung and Galena near the subway station. In uncharacteristic silence, they all boarded the train and rode it into town. Galena looked a little gray by the time the train finally rolled to a stop.

Jacquie grabbed her around the waist and shouldered some of her weight, "Let me help you out."

Jacquie supported her through the subway station and all the way into town. The pair of them walked over to a wall and Galena leaned heavily against it.

Galena looked at the concern in Jacquie's eyes, "Don't worry about me, Captain. I just need a minute to catch my breath."

"You sure?"

Galena nodded tiredly and closed her eyes, "You can count on me."

Hau Hung joined them a few minutes later. "I just checked with my connection and the package is definitely here. We need to head down to the living district."

"Are you both ready?" At Jacquie's nod, he grinned over his shoulder, "Let's get this over with."

They hitched a ride on one of the public transports and rode it to the outskirts of the living district. Buildings shaped like cubes were stacked on top of other cubes that towered up from the ground to the rocky ceiling. Each stack had rails that ran along the front of each level to a staircase at the far end. The further they traveled into the section, the older, dingier and shabbier the cubes appeared.

Hung motioned and they all hopped off the transport. The housing cubes in this zone bled a rusty orange from the dust that fell from the roof. Most of the building lights were either burned out, broken or simply missing. They followed him into one of the tiny alleys between the buildings and he pointed toward a large one across the street.

"Alright ladies, this is where you earn that extra mazuma you signed up for. I need you to retrieve the contents of a small box from the data broker, Leda Manousos. Her office is on the third level in cube Three Delta. You can find me in that surge shop across the way."

"Wait," Jacquie objected. "Aren't you going in with us?"

He just chuckled, gave a slight bow and walked away. Jacquie struggled to control her irritation as he disappeared into the surge shop.

Surge shops were a mainstay of the entire human universe. They sold beverages that featured an energy boost. Laws on various planets kept some chemical types out of their citizen's hands, but every one of them contained the old standby, caffeine.

Galena gripped the Captain by the shoulder, "Why are we doing this, again?"

"Because it's a lot of mazuma." At Galena's less than accepting frown, Jacquie explained, "We might get a lead to Lu out of it."

"Good enough for me."

The Lieutenant straightened her back as she stepped into the road and walked toward the other side. A moment later Jacquie followed her. By the time she crossed, Galena was already climbing the steps to the third level. Jacquie darted up the steps and almost caught up with her at the top.

"Wait, Galena!" she shouted.

Something about the Lieutenant's demeanor had changed. She stood straighter, but her movements were stiffer, unnatural. She did stop at Jacquie's command, but her green eyes seemed faded and unfocused.

Dullness distorted Galena's voice as it droned, "The mission?"

Jacquie steeled herself remembering what Galena had said earlier, "good enough for me." Maybe that was a trigger. Tentatively, Jacquie continued, "We go in and get the lead on where Luli is."

"Understood." Galena took off running toward the cube marked Three Delta.

"Damn it!" Jacquie cursed as she ran after her.

***

Anton looked down from the balcony. This was, without a doubt, a shitty part of town. Not the worst place he'd been to, though. The long flight up the stairs had taken its toll and his knees were not recovering fast enough. The slow clomp of boots against the metal stairs signaled the arrival of his friend as he came up to join him.

Anton glanced at the bounty hunter as he made his way to the door, "Derain, don't worry. I got this."

"You sure?" Derain leaned heavily into the wall, "By all that's holy, what is the standard gravity on this rock?"

"2-G," answered Anton as he beat out a pattern on the pressed plastic of the door. "Just look like you're going to kick everyone's ass."

"What?"

"Yeah, like that," replied Anton.

Derain grimaced, "I didn't do anything."

Anton clapped him on the shoulder and smiled broadly, "You always look like that."

A gruff voice came from the other side of the door, "Who's there?"

"We have a rendezvous with your employer, Leda Manousos," answered Anton.

The door opened and the face of a woman who had lived a hard life stood there, "My apologies, citizen. Please come in."

Derain raised an eyebrow at Anton. Anton responded with a smirk, "Please, bodyguard. Make sure it is safe."

"Bodyguard?" muttered Derain. "Is that how we're playing this?"

The bounty hunter pulled his shoulders back and pushed through the doorway. The office was appointed cleanly. Decorative shelves hung on one wall and a large, serviceable desk lay at the end of the room. A woman sat behind the desk while two other toughs stood guard in the room.

Anton peeked his head in, "Is it safe?"

"Safe enough," replied Derain.

"Please, do come in, your eminence," said the woman behind the desk.

Derain mouthed, 'Your eminence?'

Anton shrugged and wandered into the office. The hard-faced woman shut the door behind them and stood at attention. Derain followed Anton to the desk and took up position behind him.

Anton tapped the desk, "Leda, Leda, Leda... I need something special and have heard you're the one to get it for me. Is that true?"

Leda smiled as she clasped her hands

together, "Depends on what it is. I have been known to ferret out those things that are hard to find."

"I am looking for the Demetrius."

Leda's expression blanked and then she took a deferential tone, "The Demetrius? Why would someone as lustrous as yourself have anything to do with those pirates?"

"It is strange the circles one can find oneself in," answered Anton. He slipped free a surprisingly large bundle of mazuma from his pocket, "Can you help?"

Leda's eyes nearly bulged out of her head at the wad in his hand. "Of course! Let's do away with these unnecessary pleasantries. Please, come back here to join me for a drink."

Anton crowed, "Ooh! What do you have?"

***

The Lieutenant turned on a dime and slammed full force into the door. It popped off its hinges as she barreled into the main room. Gunfire erupted, followed by screams and shouting. A bullet shattered against the door frame as Jacquie entered the room. She watched in shock as Galena grabbed a woman, whose scream was cut short as her body was thrown against a desk. Two vaguely familiar males flattened themselves against the back wall, while everyone else sprawled out on the floor.

Jacquie shouted, "Lieutenant! Lieutenant! Stand down!"

"Mission completed?" came that same monotone voice.

"Uh... yes. The mission is completed."

Galena nodded and dropped to her knees. She looked up and her voice rang with life, "Jacq? Something... something is wrong." Her back arched unnaturally and vomit exploded from her mouth until she shuddered and slumped to her side.

All eyes were riveted on the Lieutenant. Jacquie whipped out her pistol and kept it pointed at the two men in the back, "You two! Drop your weapons!"

One of them piped up, "That you, Jacq?"

"Rabbit?"

"Yeah... me and Derain."

"Why the hell are you here, Captain?" asked Derain. "Actually, how did you get here?... And what made you come?"

Jacquie whistled in relief and holstered her pistol. "It's good to see you two, but no time for a reunion. Anton, help out the Lieutenant. Derain, check on the survivors. See what you can get out of them. They might know where Luli is. Keep an eye out for a small wooden box, too."

'*We're finally back together, except for Luli,*' thought Jacquie. "Well, and Barney. No one to blame for that, but me."

Anton stepped over the body of a comatose woman he had spoken to only moments ago. Galena continued to dry heave as he approached her. "Let's get you out of here, Lieutenant." He bent down and scooped her up, "I'm taking her back to the ship, Jacq."

Jacquie nodded, "Be careful with her. She's uh, not been herself of late."

"I can tell." He half supported Galena out onto the landing and they disappeared around the corner.

Jacquie gave the room a quick once over, but didn't see the package anywhere. Derain propped up Leda and began interrogating her. She was in shock. This whole side operation had gone rather poorly.

Derain shouted, "What am I looking for again?"

"A small wooden box."

Derain shook the woman by her shoulders. She pointed to a shelving unit across the room, then slumped to her side. "I think she's out cold."

Jacquie found the container after she pushed a few items off the shelf, "Got it." She peeked inside and a data card rested on its edge. With the box in hand, she headed for the door, "Let's get out of here."

The two of them left the cube and hurried down the stairs. Once they got to the street level, Derain reached out and stopped her, "What brought you here, Jacq?"

She scanned the street in front of the surge shop looking for Hung. "I took a job that promised a lead on Lu. What about you?"

"We were tracking a lead to find the crew of a ship called the Demetrius. Apparently, they do business with that bunch all the time."

"I'm going over there," she pointed, as she stepped out into the road. "The Demetrius, huh? Where'd you get that name?"

Derain hurried to keep up, "Anton caught the crew dumping Yannick's corpse. You remember him?"

"Yeah." Her eyes clouded for a moment. He had been a sweet man the couple times they had met. "Did you get any useful information?"

"Not much. We hadn't been there long before the Lieutenant burst in." He leaned in and whispered in her ear, "All I got was that they come here frequently. The woman thought they had their operation set up somewhere in the system."

"At least we're in the vicinity."

Derain blew out a pent-up breath, "Yeah... well... unfortunately, that vicinity is a lot bigger than just this planet or this system. I watched the Demetrius wormhole out."

They were making progress in these matters like players in some crazy card game; every time they held a winning hand, the rules changed.

Jacquie was fairly snarling as she approached the surge shop. She burst through the doors, stomped over to Hau Hung and slammed the small wooden box onto the table beside him.

"Here you go, Mr. Hau. Now what?"

Alarm writ itself large across his face. He grabbed the box, stuffed it under his jacket and stood up in one swift motion. He grabbed the Captain's arm and tried to pull her through the door. But to Hung's surprise, Derain stood before him, blocking the way. "Hatchet-man!" he screeched as he tried to slip past the bounty hunter. But Jacquie stopped Hung with a sharp elbow to his side that knocked him to the floor.

"This isn't the best place to talk, especially now," Derain said as he pointed out the front door to the flashing lights that reflected off the cubes.

She glanced out the window, "Right. Let's go then."

Jacquie grabbed one arm while Derain grabbed the other and they lifted Hung out through the door and into the alley. "Let's head back to the ship. We can get what we need out of him there, with no witnesses."

"Agreed," answered Derain. "Come along Mr. Hau."

***

Anton supported the Lieutenant

through the cargo hold and into the sickbay. Somewhere on the trip to the Matilda, the bandage on Galena's head had slipped off. The wound underneath had stopped seeping and an ugly new scar ran along her hairline. The gray pallor to her skin began to fade and she seemed more herself.

"Hey Doc, can you scan her?" asked Anton.

Galena muttered as she flopped onto a table, "I just had one a few hours ago. Is that really necessary?" Seeing the concern on Anton's face, she acquiesced.

The medical report Doc gave him was similar to the one he had given to Jacquie earlier. The only new revelation was that Galena's illness had been a reaction to the drugs in her system. The chip in her brain was attempting self-repair, but only time would tell how successful that might be. Doc was injecting a different drug cocktail into Galena when Jacquie and Derain entered the sickbay with Mr. Hau.

"Hau Hung!" Anton shouted as he stepped forward with his arms outstretched.

Hung grinned from ear to ear as he hugged Anton, "Quite well, thank you. You still traveling with these lunatics?"

Anton stepped back, "Not always by choice. What the hell are you doing out here?"

"About to be interrogated," interrupted Derain.

"Uh, okay. Take it easy on him,"

Anton winced at the stony expressions both Derain and Jacquie wore. "Is it alright if I bring the Cyclops on board, Captain? My departure time is coming up and I'll have nowhere to dock."

"Sure." She gave him a slight nod, "Be quick about it."

He threw her an ingratiating salute before he headed back through the airlock. Derain snorted in amusement while he dragged Hung into the lift.

"Jacq, wait up," said Galena as she slipped in next to Derain.

Once the lift rumbled to a stop on the second deck, Jacquie and Derain stepped off with Hung in tow. The Captain turned and stared deeply into Galena's eyes, "Get some rest, Lieutenant."

Galena looked as if she might protest, but then she thought better of it, "Sir, yes sir." She saluted and rode the lift up to her quarters on the third deck.

Hung lamented, "Can't we do this without the beating? After all, I'm just the messenger!"

Derain wrestled Mr. Hau into a sitting position on the weight bench and immobilized him with a few well-placed restraints. The bounty hunter stepped back to admire his handiwork, while Jacquie paced back and forth with her arms crossed. But, now and again, she would pause to press the fingers of her right hand against her forehead.

Frustration furrowed her brow as she came to a stop in front of their prisoner. "What am I going to do with you, Hung?" She began to pace again. Derain leaned against the bulkhead behind their prisoner. "What am I going to do with you?" she repeated as she grabbed his wrists. He withered under her gaze. "What's on the data card, Hung? Who wants it? Who told you they might know where Luli is?"

She pushed away from him, "I will see what's on the card, but I need to know who wants it and why. Do you understand?"

Hau Hung sat there like a whipped pet. He could sense the assassin behind him was slightly out of range. He'd heard rumors about this psycho. If he escaped his restraints, he knew that Derain would hurt him to subdue him. There would be no other option. How Jacquie could travel with someone like that was beyond him.

"I can give you the coordinates for the trade, but that's about all I know." He gulped as the shadow of the bounty hunter grew closer, "I don't know what's on the data card, because I don't care! I don't know why he wants it or what he knows about Luli Qing."

"He? Who is he? Tell me!" shouted Jacquie.

Mr. Hau's eyes grew large as they searched the darkness for an emerging presence. Radiating fear, he whispered, "I don't dare say his name."

Jon Gray Lang

Derain shouted, "By the Ghost of Tom, it's Mr. Leon isn't it?" He shook Hung by the shoulder, "Isn't it?" He snorted, "I swear that man is involved in damn near everything."

Jacquie visibly relaxed, which freaked out Hung more than anything else, "You... you both know him? Well, I guess that's some sort of relief. The instructions were pretty straight forward. Get on board the Matilda, head to Baal Shamin and steal the data card. Then convince you guys to take me to some random point in space to hand it over."

Derain muttered, "He asked for us by name?"

Hung twisted around to glance over his shoulder, "Well, not you per se, just this ship. He said you would be looking for someone and that he might have an answer by the time I returned with the data card."

"How'd he know that Luli would be missing?" groused Jacquie.

Hung babbled, "With the gossip that deep spacers are turning up dead or missing, it just made sense that she would be the one. You're loyal, Jacq. More loyal to your people than anyone else I've ever known. You wouldn't toss any of your people aside... no matter what."

At these words, Jacquie felt a pang in her heart. She felt Derain watching her with accusation in his eyes. And finally, she was glad that Anton was off the ship; she couldn't deal with that argument right now.

Jon Gray Lang

Hung rambled off into the air, "So, it had to be Luli you were looking for. Had to be her."

***

Clearance to leave the planet's surface was granted and the Matilda made its way off-world. The Cyclops was snuggly parked in the hangar bay and Anton was up on the bridge with both the Captain and Lieutenant. The coordinates provided by Hung were locked into the nav console. Fortunately, the rendezvous point just happened to be less than a day's ride in this system.

Jacquie looked down at the data card in her hand, "So much grief for this small thing."

She thought back to Derain's reaction when he realized the rendezvous location was roughly the same place where the Demetrius had disappeared through its wormhole. Loss shown in his eyes before he swallowed it up and hid the emotion away.

It had been a unanimous decision that no unnecessary chances would be taken for this meeting. The Waratah flew escort off the starboard side of the Matilda. Anton had wanted to do the same with the Cyclops, but Jacquie had asked him to stay on board as she surreptitiously pointed to Galena. He had gotten the message.

There hadn't been much on the data card. It only contained delivery manifests to a planetoid in one of the primary systems of

Consortium controlled space. None of them had ever heard of the planetoid and it didn't appear in their star charts for the Malina system.

As the Matilda cruised closer to the rendezvous point, the comm crackled open, "Copperhead to Matilda; are you there Matilda? Matilda, please reply."

"Matilda to Copperhead; this is the Matilda," answered Anton. "Requesting permission to connect."

A familiar masculine voice came through the comm, "Permission granted, Matilda. We look forward to this meeting."

After the two freighters equalized their spins, it was short work to get the airlocks lined up and connected.

Once the airlock on the Matilda was opened, Captain Kahn asked, "May we come aboard, Captain?"

Jacquie replied, "You and your crew are welcome, Captain. You as well, Mr. Leon."

Once the formal ship greetings were completed, genorgs poured in from the Copperhead. They were closely followed by Captain Ariel Kahn and Mr. Leon. The soldiers unstrapped the cargo from DV2665.1 station and began hauling it onto the Copperhead. Omega stepped free of her soldiers and headed over to Jacquie.

Omega saluted, then proffered her hand, "Captain, it is good to see you."

Jacquie smiled warmly and shook

hands with her, "It is good to see you too, Omega. Are you in charge of this bunch?"

"Yes ma'am, I am." Omega turned to address Galena, but caught sight of a slight shake of the head from Mr. Leon, "Health to you, Lieutenant." She nodded, then stepped back into the moving mass of genorgs.

Captain Kahn extended her hand, "Captain Delahaye, I am glad to see you alive and well. The last time we saw your ship, she was a bit of a wreck."

"We've had much smoother sailing of late, by Tom. Would you care for a drink? The Gods know I need one." Jacquie waved her toward the med lab and Ariel followed.

Jacquie popped open the cold storage unit and pulled out a bottle of clear liquid. "No whiskey today, I'm afraid. Is Rocket Fuel all right?"

"The cheapest hooch in all the known systems? How could I possibly say no to that?" laughed Ariel.

Jacquie laughed along with her as she poured some of the liquor into two metal tumblers, "That's good, because I can't drink this poison by myself." She handed one over and clinked Ariel's cup, "Kampai!"

"Kampai!" shouted Captain Kahn as she drained the contents of her cup.

Both of them began coughing uncontrollably.

"Gods! It burns all the way through!"

Jon Gray Lang

gasped Ariel as she sucked in a deep breath.

"It isn't called Rocket Fuel by accident, that's for sure!" wheezed Jacquie. "How have the genorgs been treating you?"

"Those soldiers have been exemplary passengers." Ariel kept an eye on Mr. Leon until he walked away from the sickbay, "Mind if I tell you something?"

Captain Delahaye raised an eyebrow, "No, please do."

Ariel whispered, "That bastard has us shipping the genorgs out as menial laborers. We've been flying from system to system as he sells them cheap in groups of five on up to fifty. And for every sale, he wears that damn grin on his face. It makes me sick."

"I didn't think his organization operated in those circles," Jacquie rejoined. "Weirdly, we did see a lot more genorgs at DV station when we picked up this cargo. But I'm pretty sure they were robbing the place."

"Robbing a system station?"

"It was a huge operation. They were stripping it of everything of value and then paying anyone with a ship to fly it out. It makes sense he's involved. The man is unfathomable. I have no idea what he's planning," Jacquie brooded.

She looked up at Ariel's thoughtful expression, "It looks like they're almost done. Anyway, another shot for the road?"

"Another for the road then.

Kampai!"

***

Hau Hung shakily stepped forward and presented the small wooden box to Mr. Leon. With an amused expression, he accepted it and opened the lid. The data card lay nestled inside. As he closed the lid, he smiled, "Excellent work, Mr. Hau."

Hung stepped back, but visibly deflated as Mr. Leon continued, "Of course, you remain part of the cargo manifest. Please come and join us on the Copperhead."

When he didn't move, Mr. Leon waved him away, "Go along. We will finish with our arrangement later."

Mr. Leon then smiled brightly as he turned toward Anton, "Mr. Roane, it is good to see you. How nice it is that you are still traveling with the Captain and the Lieutenant."

"Good day to you, too, Mr. Leon." Anton made a sour face, "I understand you might have something for us?"

Mr. Leon forced an insincere grin, "Of course. The mazuma is being brought on board now."

Two genorgs arrived with a large crate. They set it on the decking before they turned and left. The last of the cargo was pushed into the tunnel and the cargo bay lay empty.

Jon Gray Lang

"That's it?" Anton blurted. "I was made to understand there would be something more. Something more personal?"

"Oh, yes. Of course." Mr. Leon patted at his pockets. He withdrew a small slip of paper and placed it in Anton's hand, "My apologies, Mr. Roane. I had almost forgotten."

Anton opened the slip of paper. A string of numbers was written across it in broad strokes. He flipped it over, but the backside was blank, "What's this?"

Mr. Leon clapped him on the back and said, "I recently came across the existence of a religious sect with an odd doctrine."

"A religious sect?"

Mr. Leon nodded, "Allegedly, the members believe deep spacers are heavenly angels bound within their earthly shells. And they must set those souls free, so they can be angels again. Well, something like that. Cults don't tend to follow much logic."

Anton stared blankly, "And this?"

"Why that is where you will locate their sanctum or refuge or whatever they call it. I'm sure you'll find something there that will help in your search." Mr. Leon stepped back and nodded to the two captains, "Good evening, ladies."

Ariel Kahn bid her adieu and followed him into the airlock. Jacquie plucked the slip of paper out of Anton's hand and flashed a quizzical glance to Anton, "What's this?"

"Coordinates to the temple of a cult," he replied.

"A cult that looks to release the angels trapped inside the deep spacers," Galena interjected. "They cut them free from their metal husks."

Jacquie visibly shivered, "How do you know that?"

Galena stared through Jacquie and her voice seemed to come from a long distance, "I just do."

As the hatch to the Matilda closed, Mr. Hau peered through the tiny window at Galena and compared her to Omega. He looked over to Mr. Leon and asked, "What's wrong with their drone?"

twenty-three

Queen of Hearts

Barney's initial impressions of the Demetrius didn't change when she entered the wormhole. The engines rattled fiercely, causing the entire ship to tremble and three of the gauges built into each tank erratically lost pressure.

He shook his head, "I'll be lucky, if I survive this trip."

The ship tumbled as it rolled out of its wormhole. Barney's skull struck a nearby tank and he slumped to the decking. Blearily, he shook himself as he finally came to. He heard voices coming his way and quickly rolled under the nearest tank to hide. As the voices grew louder, he pulled himself further into its shadow.

"I'm telling you, Franco, there was something strange going on back at Baal Shamin,"

Marcus complained as he entered the back area.

Franco guffawed and slapped him on the back, "You're just paranoid because Orisa won't give you the time of day." Marcus stopped and turned, "No, that's not it. That's not it at all!" He leaned in, "I swear someone was following us."

"Was she pretty?" Franco smirked.

Marcus growled and headed over to the comm station. "Just shut up, Franco."

Franco began to whistle a familiar tune, then sang,

"Space is such a lonely place
all the stars around it race,
Like the beating heart of a lonely man
trapped inside a small tin can."

Marcus pointedly ignored him. In routine fashion, he engaged the comm system, "Demetrius to Polypheme, do you copy? Demetrius to Polypheme, do you copy?"

Franco continued to sing the same little ditty and danced suggestively around the room with an imaginary partner.

Marcus threw him a dirty look, then turned back to the comm, "Demetrius to Polypheme, do you copy? I repeat, do you copy?"

Franco stopped dancing and punched Marcus on the shoulder, "I bet he's not answering because he's too busy breaking the cyborg. I don't know why he won't let us just peel her open, pull the core and be done with it."

Marcus hung the microphone back on

its hook and turned off the comm, "You know why. The Masters said not to. Anyway, we tried that. She's not built like the others."

"Yeah, yeah," Franco murmured in response. "I still think the Masters should let us have another crack at her."

"Maybe they will," Marcus muttered as he turned around and punched Franco squarely in the face.

Franco staggered backward as blood exploded from his nose. His hands reached up to the ruin and his reproachful look reflected his pain.

"That's for the fucking song. I told you if you sang it again, I'd make you bleed." He spun Franco around by the shoulder and pushed him back toward the bridge, "Next time, listen to what I say. Got it? Alright, let's get you to the medkit."

Barney stayed hidden until the two of them left. Once they were out of earshot, he slid out from under the tank. He pulled himself up feeling grateful. Being small had its payoffs. From what he'd just heard, there was a good chance that Luli was still alive, too.

His hands curled into fists of determination to get Luli out of here. To his knowledge, he was the only one close enough to rescue her. "But one shouldn't lose hope that more could be out there. Now, what can I do to draw someone closer to help out?"

Then his eyes lit on the comm

station, "If I overload every frequency, someone might come to investigate!"

***

Derain brought the Waratah back on board the Matilda once the Copperhead steered its way toward the jump gate.

The comm opened up, "Once you've got her locked down, join us on the bridge, Derain."

"On my way."

Jacquie tapped her finger on the comm. Although it felt good to have Anton and Derain back, the two missing friends made her heart ache. Anton flopped into an open chair as Galena slipped into the pilot's seat.

"So, what have we got?" Derain asked as he strolled in and finished buckling on his gun belt.

"Coordinates," Anton said, as he finished keying them into the nav station. "And they lead here."

Galena studied the nav screen. "Where is that?" she asked.

Jacquie stared at the spot far past the edge of the star chart, "That would be the middle of nowhere."

Derain moved in closer as everyone peered over Anton's shoulders. Anton flipped through the other star charts, but there was no correlation.

Jon Gray Lang

"Jacq is right," Anton agreed. "That is the middle of absolutely nowhere. No jump gates feed anywhere near it. It would take months for a ship on sublight to get there."

"A wormhole drive could get there quickly," Derain advised. "Which they have."

"That's it then." Jacquie stepped back and pondered, "Best case scenario, Luli's a captive and we go in like gangbusters. Worst case scenario, it's just a wild goose chase and she's gone forever." She gave them each a look, "Thoughts?"

Galena caught Anton flashing a meaningful glance to Derain who returned it. '*What were those two scheming?*'

Anton jumped in, "I say we go for it. It's the best lead we've got."

"It's the only lead we've got," Derain corrected.

Galena watched the byplay between them, "I say we check it out. We don't have much to lose."

Jacquie met their determined looks with one of her own. "Agreed. We don't know what's waiting for us out there. If it's a bunch of religious nuts as Mr. Leon was saying, it'll be a fight."

Everyone nodded in consensus.

"Lieutenant, go warm up the jump engine," the Captain ordered. "We don't know what we're facing. Derain? I need you back on your ship. Anton, stay ready in the Cyclops."

Galena shot out of the hatch and

hopped onto the lift. Derain and Anton both ran toward the hangar bay airlock and left Jacquie standing alone on the bridge.

Jacquie stared at the star chart as her hands rolled into fists. "If you're there, we'll get you back, my friend."

***

Luli's body was laid out flat on the decking of the Polypheme. Her systems slowly came back online and her eyes flicked open. She searched for the creatures that had appeared like nightmares, but there was nothing to see from this angle. She slowly shifted and saw Jarl standing with his back against the wall.

Amused, he watched her move, "Aah, Luli. You have come back! You have returned to us. I was afraid the Masters might have taken you..."

He kept a watchful eye on her as she slowly pushed herself to her feet. She stretched out her legs and shoulders. When she flexed her fingers, she cried out from the seething pain in her broken digits. She glared at Jarl and hoped he could feel the heat of her wrath clear across the room.

"It's strange the choices one makes throughout their life, isn't it?" he bantered offhandedly. "Your decision caused a ripple effect and my decision made the ripples wider." He waved his hand to punctuate his words, "On and on it goes. Decisions... choices... with only silent moments in between." His arm, forgotten, drifted to his side.

Luli stretched her neck and the pop it made ricocheted around the room. As she surveyed her situation, her infrared system scanned the room and hallway. No sirens sounded. No one came to check on her. '*We must be alone now... it's just you and me.*' That tempered thought lit a fire of determination behind her eyes as she strode toward Jarl.

"But those moments of silence are when revelations happen!" Madness burned in Jarl's eyes as he droned on, "And all the pieces fall into place! Those precious moments when you cannot hear the music. When you should be listening... with your heart. And the pattern becomes clear! Don't you see it?"

"No. I don't," she replied as she came to a stop in front of him. "I only see an old friend who lost his mind in a piece of floating garbage in the ass-end of space."

He shook with laughter as he mashed the button on the remote that never left his hand. No response came. He pushed the button harder, then cried out in fear, "How are you still standing?" She smacked the remote from his hand, and it shattered against the decking. Tiny shards of the control device exploded outward and glittered in the air.

Suddenly, a violent impact shook through the hull of the ancient ship. A cacophony of clangs and clanks rang through the corridors and collided with thunderous rumbles coming from the floors and walls.

"It's now or never," Luli howled. She balled her misshapen hands into fists and her lips pulled away from her teeth in a rictus of agony. Her left hand shot out to grip the front of his jacket as she cocked back her right hand, poised to strike.

Jarl's brow wrinkled in confusion as he looked down at the crippled grip on his jacket, "It makes no sense. Surely, you must see them. Why else would you be chosen?" He glared at her, but then his visage softened, "But what can I say? I thought it was me. I couldn't see them at first, either."

The screech of metal grinding against itself echoed down the hallway.

Luli stepped away and looked behind her, "See what? What don't I see?" Wetness spattered her hand and wrist, and she spun to confront her tormentor.

In resignation, Jarl had jammed a small knife into the hollow under his chin. Luli's hand opened of its own volition to release his jacket. Jarl slid sideways down the wall, sputtering and choking on his own blood. In horror and confusion, Luli stared at the blood on her hand as he died.

Jon Gray Lang

twenty-four

Caught Somewhere in Time

Galena slid open the hatch to the cramped engine room. She entered the chamber, carefully worming her way around Barney's partially finished projects scattered across the work counter. A layer of dust coated every surface she touched.

"It feels deserted," she whispered.

She felt extremely heavy as the strong gravitational forces from the engine pulled at her core. A pulse spiked through her skull and a red droplet splashed against the back of her hand. She wiped at the trickle of blood that leaked from her nose, "Now is not the time!"

Galena dragged herself over to the engine's cradle. Her fingers searched for the data pad Barney had hardwired into it. She thought back to the last time she had seen him in here and concentrated on his keystrokes. On her second attempt, she accessed the data. The engine began to glow of its own volition. She could feel the engine tug at her greedily as the gravitational pull increased.

She keyed the comm, "I've got the engine online. We can jump."

"Good to hear, Lieutenant," Jacquie replied. "Stay down there and keep an eye on things."

"Understood, Captain. Galena out." She squeezed herself into the too-small seat and locked the harness in place.

The words "Preparing to jump" came through the comm loud and clear. "...in three ...two ...one ...Jump!"

The stench of molten copper and rotting fruit flooded from the spheroid into the engine room. She tried to focus on other things, but the pull on her mind was too strong. Against her will, her eyes stared at the roiling colors of the orb. Forms moved within it and slowly their faces turned around to stare back at Galena. Her skull felt as if it would split.

The comm uttered, "And we're in the mess."

Fear gripped Galena as the shadows of creatures oozed from the engine. Ghostly tentacles writhed outward and slithered across the decking. She watched in horrified fascination as they snaked through the hatch and into the main shaft.

The sensation of tiny feet tingled

across her face. She shook violently to dislodge whatever it was. It clung to her momentarily before it fell into her lap. Sweat beaded across her forehead as she watched the insectoid's legs scratch at the air. The creature's substantiality was thin, but it certainly seemed real. Strange plant life blossomed around the base of the sphere reacting to a wind she could almost feel.

Fear gripped her and she fumbled with the harness clip. When it came loose, she shook herself free and jumped up from the chair. The engine room expanded outward and she fell to her knees. Her senses tingled wildly, and she couldn't escape the feeling that there was a presence behind her. She rolled over and scooted away. The engine had become the iris of an enormous eye. The eyelid closed as it blinked at her.

"Sister? Sister? Sister, sister, sister, sister?" echoed around her. Her heart beat faster as one genorg after another flowed through the walls and surrounded her. Each one had ashen skin and eyes black as starless space. Galena backpedaled and bumped against a pair of legs. She glanced up, then tried to look away as quickly as possible. Too late, she'd already seen the distorted genorg face staring down at her.

"What is happening to me?" she cried out. "Why are you here?" Her fear was palpable, "Why can't you leave me alone!"

An unsettling feeling of loss filled the room, "We are always here with you. Forever and ever and ever..."

***

Insubstantial tentacles reached through the metal skin of the Matilda and snaked their way toward the ship's brain housing. With wet sucking sounds, they glittered on the edge of percipience. They slithered through the protective plates and flowed along the circuitry carved into her boards. Like digits exploring something once known but now forgotten, they poked and prodded their way into the machine that was the mind of the ship. Matilda's mind lost the battle and the beast took over.

The invading tentacles gradually thickened and increased in substantiality. The whole of the ship bucked in revolt as its journey continued through the 'other space'. What remained of the ship's systems began to fluctuate wildly.

***

The Matilda thrashed her way back into normal space, tumbling recklessly until the actuators leveled her out. Galena was violently thrown against the ceiling of the engine room before she rebounded against the work counter. She lay quite still on the decking. Her mouth remained in a grimace as her eyes stared blankly at her surroundings.

Jon Gray Lang

"And we're clear," came the most welcome words ever spoken over the comm.

twenty-five

Destroy Everything You Touch

The Independence pulled away from the Silk Road and tore the boarding tunnel from its moorings. As the remnants of the tunnel connection broke free, it fluttered in the solar winds and slammed against the station.

Commander Keri trembled in the pilot seat. Her hands were noticeably unsteady and dark rings encircled her eyes. Mr. Leon had patched her wounds well enough for her to initiate their departure. Now he forced her to swallow a couple of stim tabs to keep her from passing out.

"We've got confirmation from the jump gate. Cat's Eye is locked and loaded in the nav system. Can someone take over? I need to lay down," Rosa grunted.

"Rho-11! Take over piloting. You

two, take the Commander to sickbay," barked Delta.

Rosa shakily stood up and was immediately assisted by a couple soldiers.

After the Commander left the bridge, Delta turned to Mr. Leon, "I like that one. She is one of the few good natural-borns."

"She is that," Mr. Leon agreed. "If you'll excuse me, I wish to see to her in sickbay."

Delta stood at attention and saluted. Mr. Leon caught himself returning her salute and laughed at his blunder. One of the offhand remarks from Dr. Saric came to his mind, "The longer you stay with them, the more you'll pick up their habits." He chuckled again at the memory.

Entering the sickbay, he found Rosa lying in an open med tube, attended by one of the genorg medics who checked her bandages.

"How is she?" asked Mr. Leon.

"She will live. She just needs time to recover," replied the medic as she left him alone with the patient. Mr. Leon looked down at Rosa and her color looked as if it might be returning.

"Ms. Keri? Can you hear me?" There was no response. He shook her lightly, "Can you hear me, Rosa?"

She stirred at his touch and her eyes opened wide. "Was the tea salvageable? I would hate for it to go to waste."

Rex laughed and took her hand, "Oh yes my dear. The tea is quite alright. Once you are on your feet, I will make you a cup. Maybe I will tell you a story... or maybe I will speak of my dreams and desires."

"That would be nice," she said as the pain killers kicked in. She drifted away and her hand grew limp in his.

"I am overjoyed that you decided to work for me, Ms. Keri." His hand drifted to his side as he gazed at her face, "I feel I might be able to trust you. I want to trust someone and tell them my plans for the future, but I simply can't on blind hope."

***

The door to Dr. Wyeth's berth chimed three times before she said, "Please, come in."

Yeoman Fitzpatrick opened the door, then looked furtively down the hallway in both directions. Once he thought it was clear, he stepped into the Doctor's cabin and closed the door behind him.

He came to attention, "You asked for me?"

"I did," she replied from her perch on her desk. "I enjoyed your attention to detail during your interrogation of the Tiwi clan. You handled yourself like a professional."

Fitzpatrick blushed, "Oh, thank you, Dr. Wyeth. I enjoy that class of assignment. It's kind of a passion for me."

"I could tell. Why don't you take a seat, Yeoman? I have something important to discuss with you."

The Yeoman gave a slight bow and swiveled out the desk chair. He settled into it, leaned forward and rested his forearms on his knees. "What can I do for you, ma'am?"

The Doctor smiled lightly, "Where do you see yourself in five years, Mr. Fitzpatrick? In ten?"

"I want to command a ship of my own but that'll take longer than ten years."

"Yeoman, may I call you, Harrison?"

"I would be honored."

"What would you say to the command of a ship in less than two years?"

"That would be wonderful, but I don't see how that's possible."

Dr. Wyeth smiled, "I can make that happen for you, but I would need you on my side."

"My loyalties lie with the Senai Family," Harrison replied. "If it doesn't hurt them, what would you need me to do?"

"Captain Kaplean has become a thorn in my side and I may need to wrest control from his hands. I am looking for allies."

"The Captain seems to be a good man but better than my own command?" He shrugged, "I think not."

Dr. Wyeth smiled, "Excellent, excellent. Welcome to the team, Yeoman

Fitzpatrick. We shall do great things together."

***

Jacquie scanned the cosmic area. There was very little out here besides dust; not a single rock big enough to land on. She ran the scans again and again, but they all came back the same.

"Gods be damned!" she shouted. "There's nothing here!" Her hands clenched in fear and frustration. "What are we going to do? I don't know where else to look!"

The comm lit up and Derain's voice came through, "You see anything out there, Jacq?"

Her eyes moistened at the corners even as she slammed them shut to stop the tears. She growled and wiped furiously at her eyes. Sighing heavily, she keyed the comm, "No. I don't see a damn thing." Her eyes focused on the outer comm channels. They were spiking like mad, "Wait."

She switched the comm to all the frequencies and rolled through each one. There was nothing but various bands of static, yet they all came from a single point of origin. Hope rekindled as she re-calibrated the scanners for a longer, more focused search. She almost crowed in delight as a small gravitational body appeared on the outer edge.

She set the nav computer and kicked the sublight engines on. Once the Matilda was moving, she commed back, "I think I found something. Stay ready."

Jon Gray Lang

As they sailed closer to the object, her heart began to beat faster. She bounced scans all over the object as the Matilda pieced together what was out there. A long ship assembled from random parts was docked against a much larger frigate. The static on the comm channels came from the elongated vessel. She singled it out and tight beamed it over to the Waratah.

"Does the smaller ship look familiar, Derain?"

"That's the Demetrius, alright. It's connected to a monster of a frigate, but I've never seen one like it before. It must be ancient."

"Should I exit the hangar bay?" Anton asked.

While the Matilda grew closer to the mystery ship, Jacquie continued to scan both it and the Demetrius. The comm channels were swamped with static, otherwise there was no response to their presence.

She commed back to Derain and Anton, "No. We don't know which ship Luli might be on. They haven't noticed us, so we'll do this one quietly."

twenty-six

Fairies Wear Boots

The Matilda slipped in close to the frigate. Docking ports littered the starboard side but many of them looked damaged beyond use. She kept searching for an open docking port and spied one with working lights. She lined up the Matilda's cargo bay airlock with it and popped the attitude jets until the two ships matched rotations.

Jacquie extended the airlock tunnel. When it registered a successful connection to the docking ring, she blew out a tense breath and ran her palm across her forehead, "Whew... so far, so good." She commed to the Waratah, "Derain, go ahead and come back in. I want you and Rabbit to sneak aboard the Demetrius. See if they left someone behind."

"On my way."

Jon Gray Lang

Jacquie commed the engine room, "Lieutenant, you there?"

There was a long delay, but eventually, Galena's tired voice commed back, "Here, Captain."

A part of Jacquie relaxed a bit, "Meet me in the cargo bay. We're going to board that thing. You can consider anyone on it to be a threat. Got it?"

There was an unsettling change in Galena's voice, "Understood, Captain. Lieutenant out."

***

"I hate these grab-n-go tactics, especially when we go in blind," Anton grumbled.

Derain thumped him in the chest as he cycled open the hangar bay doors, "Quit your bitching and be ready."

The two men quickly linked their spacesuits together and waited on the hangar bay doors to open. Once they were opened wide enough, they stepped outside onto the launch pad that ran the length of the main shaft.

They carefully approached the old frigate where both the Matilda and the Demetrius were docked. The frigate glowed with a sickly greenish aura that, luckily, illuminated their way. The Demetrius was stationed a couple of docking rings over.

"I think I see a hatch," offered Anton.

Derain asked, "You sure?"

"Sure as I can be from out here."

"Good enough for me," replied Derain. "Lead the way."

Together, they lined up with the hatch and launched themselves off the pad toward it. Derain tapped at the controls for his suit jets and their travel path adjusted accordingly. The minutes passed in silence. When they drew close enough to the Demetrius, Anton fired a compressed gas gun loaded with a spear tip. The tip, trailed by a cable, launched toward the heavily scarred vessel. Once it slammed into the hull, Anton reeled in the duo.

"Wish we'd had that when we pulled you off the Vogelgesang," Derain reminisced.

Anton cracked a smile, "I've traveled long enough with Jacq to always keep one on hand."

Derain's laughter echoed through the comm. They activated their magnetic boots and clamped onto the surface of the hull. Anton pried the spear tip loose, spun the cable tight and holstered the gun. They moved over to the hatch that protruded from the pitted surface of the hull.

The hatch was old and corroded. As they pounded at the lock, chips of metal rot floated away. Suddenly, the wheel spun freely. Then weapons in hands, they slipped through the open hatch with Derain in the lead.

The airlock was small and empty. Anton closed the outer door as Derain activated the pressurization sequence. The indicator light changed from a rusty red to a faded green and the inner hatch popped open. They moved gingerly into an empty room that had seen its fair share of death. Blood was splashed across the walls and the floor where a strange altar stood guard in the center of the chamber.

"Do I want to know what they did in here?" Anton murmured into the comm.

"No, I'm pretty sure you don't." Derain gagged as his thoughts filled with gruesome memories of his family's butchered bodies. Without warning, he turned and grabbed the front of Anton's suit, "You remember our deal?"

"Uh, which one?" Anton asked. Derain shook him vigorously. He gulped as he looked around, "Uh, yeah. The one to be paid at some future time, right?"

"Exactly." Derain released him and marched toward another on the far side of the room.

"Do you want to use that favor now?" Anton squeaked.

Derain chuckled darkly, "No. I just needed to make sure you remembered."

"What brought that on?" Anton muttered under his breath.

They opened the second hatch and walked into a worse mess. What was left of a barrel-chested man lay broken on the decking. His skull had been crushed. Metal glimmered through the twisted remnants of the girders that had once held a fuel tank against the bulkhead. Evidently, a powerful force had yanked at the tank until it snapped and fell on the victim.

"Hell of a way to go," quipped Anton.

Derain placed a single finger over Anton's faceplate and then pointed to an open hallway beyond the piles of radio gear. He stepped into the corridor and Anton stuck close behind him. They passed an empty cabin, then discovered another body laying halfway through the next doorway. Both legs and one arm were bent at unnatural angles.

Recognition lit up Anton's face, "Hey, this is one of the guys who dumped Yannick's corpse!"

Derain tapped Anton's faceplate again and raised a finger to his lips. Anton shrugged and waved Derain ahead.

The empty cockpit was a disaster. Blood was sprayed across the bow port and one of the seats had been snapped off at its base. They moved on to the main airlock.

The inner hatch was open, but the outer hatch was shut tight. A bloody handprint was smeared over the control pad. Derain scratched at the dried blood until the symbols on the pad were legible. He slipped the knife he carried back into its sheath and pulled out his pistol. Anton keyed a command into the control pad and they waited as the hatch cycled open.

Jon Gray Lang

A third body was splayed out in the docking tunnel. This man's face had been beaten in, probably with the broken armrest that lay close by. They glanced further down the tunnel.

"I'm pretty sure that's the other guy I saw dumping Yannick," Anton stated. "The Demetrius was supposed to have a crew of three and I think that's what's left of them."

"You think Barney did this?"

Anton nodded reluctantly, "I've only seen him fight for his life once before... and he broke a lot of people then... a lot of people."

"I will never piss off a Titan," muttered Derain.

***

Jacquie studied Galena with a pang of remorse. The pallid woman looked haggard, and her breathing rattled from her chest. The left side of her face had a sizable bruise. But here she was, loyal and willing to serve. And Jacquie knew she couldn't handle this mission alone. She threw a quick nod to the Lieutenant, then hit the airlock control.

The hatch parted to reveal a long empty hallway. The lighting was dim, but even so, the advanced age of the ship was apparent. She was ancient. Corrosion, most likely caused by water damage, had eaten tracks into the walls of the hallway. Dark stains of unknown origin blotted the walls and the decking.

"I smell blood, old blood," Galena's words sliced through the stillness.

A shiver ran down Jacquie's back. From the corner of her eye, she watched the Lieutenant sniff at the stale air. Galena strode forward with almost machine-like movements and Jacquie broke into a trot to keep up. As they passed an intersection, she looked down the other corridor and noticed that both ends of it had been blockaded with garbage and other detritus.

"Why would someone do that?" Jacquie wondered as she ran to catch up with her friend.

The further they advanced along the hallway, the more mechanical Galena's movements became. When the Lieutenant finally slowed down, Jacquie caught up and gently put a hand on her arm.

"We're almost there," Galena whispered as she turned to face the Captain.

Jacquie involuntarily stepped back. The genorg's green eyes were empty of their awareness and they were slowly darkening. Jacquie's heart beat faster as she brought up her pistol and took aim. She didn't know what else to do. Galena's head twisted back toward the hallway as she sniffed at the air again.

A heart-stopping scream ripped through the hallway, then suddenly cut off.

"Search the rest of the ship!" Jacquie screamed and ran off toward the scream alone, leaving the Lieutenant behind. All the while, she prayed, "Please don't let that be Luli. Please don't be Luli. Please, please... please..."

twenty-seven

Junk Satellite

Luli sawed the flap of skin away from Jarl's skull with the small knife she had pried loose from his neck. Once the flap was large enough, she pulled the skin back with a swift yank. The knife slipped from her bloodied grasp but she caught it before it clattered to the decking.

Luli winced in pain as her fingertips searched for the indentation in the metal plate. Her fingers lacked the dexterity to easily turn the switch, but she kept trying. An audible click signaled her success and a tiny smile of triumph spread across her face. Jarl Moritsson's memory core popped up and she wrested it free from its housing.

A slithering shuffle followed by a light laugh sounded behind her.

Jon Gray Lang

***

Jacquie ran with everything she had down the long hallway and turned into the room at the far end. What she saw there made her stop short. Synthetic blood pooled across the decking where Luli crouched over a twitching body. Jacquie moved slowly toward her.

"Lu? Are you okay?" She reached out a hand and touched Luli's shoulder, "What are you doing? Are you hurt?"

In one fluid movement, Luli spun around and jammed the small knife into Jacquie's thigh. She snarled as Jacquie fell backward in surprise and pain. Luli turned back to Jarl's body and pulled off the necklace of memory cores. She clicked Jarl's memory core to the necklace and slipped it over her own head. The cylinders glinted against her chest.

Suddenly, Galena set foot into the room. "The ship seems devoid of life, Captain..." her nostrils flared and she stumbled against the bulkhead. Black inkiness clouded her eyes and she shuddered.

Confusion filled Luli's blank gaze. She saw Jacquie sitting in front of her with the handle of a knife sticking out of her leg and Galena beyond her in the hatchway. The Lieutenant fell to her hands and knees, retching in spasms. A black viscous fluid poured from her mouth, nose, and eyes.

Jacquie stared in astonishment at the ragged skin peeling from Luli's exposed metal skull. What was left of her hairline was jagged and her remaining hair hung in filthy, matted wisps. Her hands appeared to be grotesquely deformed under the ragged bandages that ran from her fingertips to her elbows. Splotches of blood, both new and old, stained the remnants of her flight suit.

Luli blinked, slowly coming to her senses. "Jacq?" Luli whispered, "Are you here?" Her voice trailed off as her eyes rolled back into her head and she slumped to the floor again.

Jacquie turned around at the sound of Galena's groans.

"I don't feel right," Galena moaned as she fainted. The black fluid that oozed around her head began to bubble and melt the decking.

Jacquie grabbed at her comm and shouted into it, "Derain! Anton! Somebody, come quick! Lu's down and I've got a knife in my leg. And... and I don't know what the hell is happening to Galena!"

She tugged the small knife out, and it clattered to the decking. She tore a strip of cloth from the dead cyborg's shirt, wrapped it tightly around her wound and stumbled to her feet. With a surge of adrenaline, Jacquie dragged Luli toward the hatch where the open hallway beckoned.

She could hear heavy footsteps approaching as she struggled with Luli's comatose body. She didn't look up until she heard, "What in the nine hells happened in here?"

It was a voice from Jacquie's past, a wonderful voice that had comforted her when she was little. In the worst moments of her life, he had been there with the right words to help her move forward. She hadn't realized how much she needed him until now.

"Barney! Oh, thank the Major! See what you can do for Galena!" Jacquie stumbled and Luli's heavy body fell against her wounded leg. Jacquie squealed in pain as her bandage grew wet with new blood.

"On it, love," Barney said behind her.

He grabbed Galena by the waist and pulled upward, but the black, pungent fluid stuck to the decking and her head remained trapped in the tar-like substance. The glint from a knife blade lying on the floor caught his eye. He grabbed it and sawed at the viscous material. It parted before the blade and Galena came free.

Out in the hallway, the Captain struggled to drag Luli, but she wasn't making much progress. Barney threw Galena over one shoulder, then scooped up Luli and settled her onto his other shoulder. Jacquie gave up gratefully and slumped against the wall. Beads of sweat decorated her forehead and her breathing was labored. Barney gazed at her with deep sadness in his eyes. It hurt Jacquie to see that, so she looked away.

"Um. I'll carry these two to the sickbay on the Matilda. Which way is it?" Jacquie pointed down the left hallway but was otherwise silent. "I hope to see you there soon, Captain."

Barney's gait wasn't slowed by the weight of the two women and he quickly disappeared around a corner, eager to find an exit from this rust bucket.

Jacquie slid down the wall in silence. The full weight of her choices hit her, "Fool that I am. Time to abandon my pride for the sake of my people." She sighed, "For my sake, too."

twenty-eight

These Days

The M33 cruised through the jump gate into the DV2665 system. Captain Kaplean idly watched as his crew went through their paces. Ident requests were blocked and the chatter from the jump gate quickly dwindled to nothing. His data pad blinked with the data dump obtained automatically from the jump gate.

He flipped through the updates and muttered to himself, "The Tuls system has been quarantined, reason unknown. And these messages mention similar disturbances in unconnected systems..." His brow wrinkled in thought as he flipped through them all again. "Ms. Shimada, am I reading these updates correctly?"

"What do you mean, sir?" she asked.

"Multiple raids on outer system

mining stations committed by genorg pirates?"

Mariko correlated the news feed data by type, "Yes sir. Thirteen mining and trade stations have been raided by pirates. Eyewitness reports all say it was the work of drones... I mean genorgs. Make that fourteen. Toros Colony is now on the list."

The Captain sat back. Raids on outer system stations occurred with some frequency, but he had never heard of genorgs being the perpetrators. "Toros Colony? That's in this system, correct?"

"Yes it is, sir."

He swiped his data pad clear, "Officer Grissom? Please make for the station above Toros Colony."

"Sir, yes sir."

Shimada Mariko suddenly yelled, "Belay that order!"

Captain Kaplean grunted, "Explain yourself."

She continued, "Captain, I discovered a message request for both the Matilda and Waratah to meet in the Ankara system!"

"Who sent the message?" he asked.

She poured through her screens, "The message came from the yacht registered as Cyclops."

There was that ship again. What was its connection with the Matilda and the Waratah?

Mariko shunted a report over to his data pad, "This is a record of the Matilda requesting a permit to the Ankara system. It's only a few days old." She looked up to see his dark expression, "Uh, sir."

Captain Kaplean flicked his hand, "You heard her! Set course for Ankara."

"Sir! Yes, sir!"

***

Barney marched through the dimly lit passageways with a woman draped over each shoulder. Rounding a corner, he nearly collided with Anton and Derain.

"Took you two long enough," Barney grumbled.

"Are they...?" asked Derain.

"They're both breathing. That's all I know for certain."

Anton quipped, "Barney, I've been wondering... Did your arms get tired from punching that last guy? Is that why you switched to the armrest back there?"

"Ask me that again, but stand closer to an airlock," Barney retorted. "Good to see you, Derain. Now, out of the way," he growled. "I need to get these two to sickbay."

"No one appreciates a good pun these days," muttered Anton.

Derain stepped toward Barney, "Do you need help?"

Barney stopped and shifted the

weight on his shoulders, "I've got them, but Jacq's been stabbed in the leg. Go and give her a hand."

Derain nodded, then disappeared down the hall. Barney resumed his march toward the Matilda as Anton turned to follow him.

"Hey, Barney!" Anton shouted. "Wait up."

Barney ignored him and kept up his pace. When he stepped into the cargo bay, he felt Galena slightly slipping on his shoulder. "Damn," he grumbled as he hurried to the med lab.

Two med tubes were ready and waiting for patients as Barney entered the sickbay. He waved to the automaton, "Doc, run a scan on Luli, now... and no buts about it!"

For a change, Doc went about its task meekly and generated a diagnostic report with no fuss.

Barney scratched at his temple as he read the report. At this point, the damage to Luli's scalp was severe, but removal of the dead skin would keep the rot from spreading. Her metal frame was nicked with cuts and scratches and her organic parts were malnourished. Her erratic brain waves caused him some concern, but nothing prepared him for the report on her hands. They were destroyed.

"How does the Lieutenant look, Rabbit?"

There was a long pause as Anton brushed at her face, "Huh. The stuff on her face just flaked off. She's alive but she looks really bad. I think she has a concussion."

Luli's breathing accelerated as her eyes opened. Her hands shot up against the lid of the med tube and warning lights flashed along its case. Doc swung around and pushed Barney away.

Luli screamed, "No! Not again! Let me out!"

Barney ran to the med tube and peered through the glass, "Whoa lass, calm down." He opened the lid a crack. She tried to scurry out, but Doc extended three of his arms to pin her in place. Barney reached his hands into the case and cupped Luli's face, murmuring softly to soothe her. "It's alright. It's alright. You're on the Matilda, love," He cooed. "You're safe. You're home now."

Luli's eyes blinked a few times, "Barney? What are you doing here?"

"Why, looking after you, of course." His fingers traced the tear tracks on her cheeks, "I heard you were in a spot of trouble, so I went looking for you. We all did."

"I'm on the Matilda?" she asked. Her breathing slowed down, and her eyes stopped their frantic searching. "I am, aren't I? Oh, thank the Major."

Anton stepped over; he smiled down at her and she returned a weak smile of her own. Barney tugged on his sleeve and waved him over. Anton shrugged at Luli, then walked away to confer with Barney.

"I'm glad to see Lu is awake, but

Galena is still out cold. She looks really bad," Anton said. "So... what now?"

Barney leaned in closely, "I need you to run interference for me with the Captain, alright? She knows I'm here."

"You think she'll still be mad?" Anton asked.

Barney pursed his lips and nodded in response.

"Uh, right. I've got your back."

Anton backed away. He waved goodbye to Luli as he stepped out of the sickbay. Barney picked up the medical report for Galena and studied the findings. He gave a quizzical glance to Doc as he compared this report to an earlier one. The damaged circuitry in Galena's skull would certainly complicate her chances of a quick recovery.

"You had to hit her in the head, eh?" Barney asked.

Doc chirruped, "Du che to da me."

The Titan harrumphed at the answer. Physically, Galena was healthy, except for the concussion. She was stable for the moment. Enforced rest was about all they could do for now.

Barney considered the situation in silence, shifting his weight from one foot to the other. As he moved, an object in his pocket poked him in the leg. He reached in and pulled out the memory core. He squared his shoulders and walked back over to Luli's med tube.

"I hate to be the bearer of bad news

Lu, but your friend Yannick is dead," Barney said, as he proffered the memory core to her.

She stared at it, then closed her eyes as Barney fastened it onto the necklace. "That's it then," she whispered. "They're all dead. I'm the only one left."

Her body shook from the pain of her loss. Barney gathered her into a hug, and she sobbed into his collar. Her broken hands clutched at him as she released a torrent of pent-up emotions. Then she examined her hands and cried all the harder. "My hands... I have nothing left."

Barney lifted her chin and stared into her eyes, "I will do everything in my power and my ability to fix them, Lu." He then pulled her to him and just let her cry.

***

Derain found the Captain limping her way down the corridor. He gave her a shoulder to lean on. With a sigh, she threw her arm around his neck and sagged into his side.

"Thanks," she smiled at him. "The way back is a lot longer than I remembered."

The wet bloodstain on her pant leg glistened. "How bad is it?" Derain asked.

"I don't think its too deep, but by Tom it hurts." She attempted a smirk, but it became more of a grimace, "To be honest, I'm worried that the blade hadn't seen a cleaning in months."

Jon Gray Lang

"Doc will give you a complete checkup."

Jacquie's eyes were bright as she kept moving forward. "We did it, though," she beamed. "We found Luli and she's still alive."

twenty-nine

My House Has Wheels

The long dark spacecraft punched through the jump gate and sailed out into the Ankara system. The crew remained on high alert. They might be just a few days behind their quarry. Captain Kaplean waited patiently as Officer Shimada searched through the latest data dump for a new lead. But the only news besides another quarantined system, had been about more attacks perpetrated by genorg pirates in the outer systems.

An oddity in the whole business was that a particular name kept cropping up, Lieutenant Galena Chadov. A single person couldn't be everywhere at once. Even without solid intel on the jump capability of the Matilda, a single unknown can't defy logic.

He cycled his data pad and filtered

through the posts until he came across a report from the CBC Remus after the alien invasion in the Pequiz system. Part of the report covered the loss of over one thousand genorg soldiers, all listed as Equipment Casualties. It bothered him that they weren't classified as Missing-In-Action, but then the powers that be didn't consider them to be human.

He sighed at the discrepancy, "The trouble with bureaucracy is their pointless categories."

"Sir?" uttered Officer Shimada.

Captain Kaplean gazed at her over his console, "Yes?"

Mariko nodded quickly, "The station has entry records for the Waratah, the Matilda, and the Cyclops. All three vessels requested access to Baal Shamin."

"Hmm...," he pondered. "The Waratah, too? Anything from our team in the Aken system?"

"No sir," she softly replied.

"Are there any exit records?"

She double-checked the report, "No sir. No system exit requests under those ship names."

"Finally, some progress," muttered the Captain. "Mr. Grissom? You have your destination."

"Aye, aye sir."

"Ms. Hayley? Please inform Dr. Wyeth of our destination."

***

An armored transport from the M33 flew into the hangar on Baal Shamin and made port. As Captain Kaplean disembarked from the lander, he was quickly followed by Dr. Wyeth and an armed escort. A mercenary team from the local precinct had a train waiting exclusively for the M33's entourage. The Captain and Doctor sat as far apart as possible, while the virtually empty train slowly made its way into the city.

The precinct office was cater-cornered to the station. The team from the M33 was waived past all the security protocols and taken to the interrogation cells. Captain Kaplean looked in on the witness, Leda Manousos, as she regaled a detective with her story.

"Why do I have to tell you, again? None of it has changed!" she cried.

The detective pounded the desk, "Because it doesn't make sense. Drones are docile; they're not war machines."

Captain Kaplean could feel the creepy smile appear on the Doctor's face at those words. He ignored the sensation and continued watching the interrogation through the double sided glass.

"That one sure as hell is. Fine! The things a law-abiding citizen has to put up with these days." Leda brushed loose strands of hair to cover the lump on her forehead, "Me and my associates was entertaining a couple gentlemen when this psycho drone comes crashing through my front door! Before I even says hello, she grabs Pauley and snaps her neck against my desk. Chakrii tries to stop her and she slams him into the wall."

Captain Kaplean read over the descriptions of the gentlemen in question. One of the men matched the profile of the bounty hunter and Leda had already identified Anton Roane from his prison holo. Leda's police record listed her as an information broker of the less than legal kind. He held the report out to Dr. Wyeth, "It's her alright. The suspect identified two of her traveling companions."

The Doctor snorted, "What would my test subject need companions for? Now be quiet."

"Pauley and Chakrii are ...?" asked the detective.

Leda cleared her throat, "Uh... well, they were in my employ as bodyguards. The universe is a scary place, you know."

"Ms. Manousos, we have a handful of out-of-system warrants out for your bodyguards. Do you think perhaps the genorg was there for them?"

Leda scoffed, "No way. She and the woman with her was after some box I was holding for a client. And no, it wasn't valuable. It was only a shipping manifest."

"A shipping manifest?"

Leda nodded, "It was stored on a data card. I took a peek, you know. Kind of a grocery list, really."

The detective picked up a data pad, "Can you describe the other woman?"

"I only saw her for a second..."

"A shipping manifest, you say?" As Kaplean pondered this information, the comm chirped. "What is it?" he snapped.

"We just received confirmation that the three craft exited the planet's gravity well about an hour ago."

"Thank you, Ms, Shimada. We'll be returning shortly." He clicked the comm off, "Doctor, we have what we came for. Our quarry left the planet an hour ago."

"Then what are we standing here for? Do your damn job and get me my drone!"

"You heard the Doctor, Chief Bull. Ready the team. We're heading back."

"Understood, sir," replied the Chief. "Squad! Form up!"

The train ride back was a solemn affair. Not a word was spoken after they disembarked and headed into the station.

When the entourage passed the front desk, an attendant approached the Captain, but he barely noticed her presence. Chief Bull tapped his shoulder. He glanced up from his deep thoughts to see an older woman standing there, with the air of a matron not used to being ignored.

"Yes?" answered the Captain.

Dr. Wyeth raised an eyebrow at this delay, "I'll make sure your ship is ready for take-off, Captain. Best not be late or you just might never leave this place."

The Captain dismissed the rest of the party with a wave and they ran to catch up with the Doctor. Chief Bull stayed close to the Captain and waited.

"Captain, eh?" With no response from the man, she continued, "Your soldiers asked for departure coordinates on three ships. Is that correct?"

Hope flickered in his expression, "That is correct."

The woman gave a lascivious smile, "All three left port within an hour of each other. We caught sight of the smaller ones boarding the larger one, but we lost track of them at these coordinates." She showed him a series of numbers on her data pad.

His small flicker of hope was extinguished. So close and somehow they've eluded us once again. "Was there anything else?"

"About the three vessels?"

He sighed at the innuendo in her tone, "Anything else of importance."

"Oh." She scrolled through her data pad, "Local news is rife with the story of a deep spacer's body found in a dumpster."

"Who was it?" he asked.

She scrolled down a bit more, "Yannick Specht. Are you looking for him, too?"

He smiled at her, "No. Just mild curiosity. Bodies have been mysteriously turning up all over the place, lately." He turned to leave, then added, "Would you please send those coordinates to my ship?"

"Of course, Captain," she replied. "Pleasant journeys."

As Kaplean proceeded to the transport, Chief Bull fell in step behind him.

"Sir, do you think the genorg we're searching for is also murdering the deep spacers?" Chief Bull posited.

"To be honest Chief, it wouldn't surprise me. The coordinates are the only lead we have. Let's hope they prove useful."

thirty

Damned if She Do

The figurine in Barney's vest pocket thumped against the side of the med tube. He slipped the spaceman out and his fingers traced the lines of its suit. It had seen better days. Parts of the suit were worn down to the yellowish plastic underneath. The insignia on the shoulder retained flecks of red and blue but was not recognizable as to what it had once been. He placed the figure on top of Luli's med tube and the helmet wobbled as if sharing a secret joke. Luckily, Luli remained peacefully asleep.

Derain's voice came over the comm, "Doc, keep the Lieutenant sedated until further notice."

Doc asked, "Li do tong sa?"

Barney laughed at Derain's audible

sigh, "Captain's orders. Will you just do it?"

"Che tuu da!" replied Doc as it trundled on its track to the Lieutenant's med tube. Galena would never know what hit her.

Barney glanced up at the automaton, "Let me know if there is any change, any change at all. And no back talk, alright?"

Doc whirred at him and glided away. The engineer shook his head. He stepped out into the Matilda's cargo bay. A crew meeting had been called and to his surprise, Jacq had asked him to attend. "I can't let Jacquie boot me off now, Matilda. You have any ideas for how to keep me on board?" The ship was quiet. "Bah! Why should I ask you?"

Making his way to the ship's lounge, Barney paused at a port to gaze at the vessels they'd so recently departed. The Matilda had decoupled from the rotting hulk of the Polypheme and now floated off its starboard side. Not a living soul remained on that ancient wreck or on the Demetrius.

"Dead because they wanted her memories..." From what Luli said, they wanted a way back to Earth. He shook his head, "All that trouble for a map to a dead system."

The mood in the lounge was somber. Barney nodded to Derain and Anton as he took a seat at the table. He could feel the heat of Jacquie's eyes on him, so he kept his averted.

Jacquie cleared her throat, "Let's get this started then. Mr. de Lagnel, what's the status of the two in sickbay?"

Barney looked at the faces around the table, "Luli is recovering. Most of the damage done to her is superficial. Doc is pumping her full of fluids to combat the malnourishment." He rubbed at his brow, then continued, "As you know, her hands were broken. It... it looks like it might have been done multiple times. The bad news is the breaks have all reset. As they are now, uh, she'll never play her uke again."

Jacquie's grimace was mirrored by everyone and the room grew silent.

"Anything we can do?" Anton asked at last.

Barney looked down at his hands, "Because she is not entirely flesh and bone, a break and rebuild may not work. Doc and I are looking into other options. Aside from her hands though, Luli should be up and ready to pilot in a few days."

"What about the Lieutenant?" Jacquie asked.

"Doc is still mapping the circuitry in her skull to see how widespread the damage is," Barney replied. "The chip's nanofilaments have spread further into her brain and down her spinal cord than we had originally thought. Doc and I still don't understand how it reacts with the alien goo or why. Even worse, the goo has spread further throughout her body." His gaze met everyone's eyes, "Frankly, I don't know what to do for her except repair what we can. Will that help in the long run? I don't know."

"We'll keep her sedated for now,"
commanded the Captain. "We can't afford to have
her wandering the ship in her current state. Is there
anything else?"

Barney stood up and squared his
shoulders, "Yes. Yes, there is. Luli has requested that
we destroy both ships. She says she could sleep
easier knowing that they were nothing but dust."

"I completely agree," said Anton.

Jacquie nodded, "So do I. We'll leave
nothing for the salvagers. Now, everyone is
dismissed except you, Mr. de Lagnel."

Anton slapped his hands against the
table as he stood up. But before he could speak,
Derain grabbed him by the shoulder and led him out
of the lounge. Barney watched them as they passed
through the hatchway before he turned back to face
the Captain.

"With all due respect, I am requesting
that I be allowed to remain onboard the Matilda
until Luli is fully recovered." He rushed on before
Jacquie could interrupt, "I'm the only engineer you
have on the ship and she's going to need more than
Doc to work on her. And since we're on the subject,
I think you should keep me here until the Lieutenant
stabilizes for the exact same reasons. There now,
I've said my piece."

Jacquie gazed at him as he stood
there, stoically waiting for her to banish him again.
Part of her was still angry with him, but she had

come to accept that she needed him more. He had always been there at her side and had kept her going through all the rough times.

She walked over to Barney, took both of his shoulders in her hands and stared deeply into his eyes, "I have been a fool before, and I probably will be again. I want you to stay on the Matilda. I... I need you to stay. Besides these other misfits, you're the only family I've got." She pulled him in for a hug, "Can you forgive me?"

She could feel him relax as he pulled her in tighter. Her eyes grew misty when he muttered, "Of course, love." Suddenly, she felt at peace. Her rock had returned. As horrible as things had become, she still had her family.

She whispered, "I have missed you."

***

Luli wandered in through the bridge hatch looking exhausted, but in high spirits.

"It's good to see you up, Lu," chorused the rest of the crew.

She smiled weakly and brandished the spaceman figurine, "So... who do I owe for this favor?"

Barney grinned and blushed, "You travel enough, you pick up a few souvenirs. It seemed to suit you."

She plopped the figurine on top of the pilot's station and slid into the seat, "Okay, little starman... let's get this done!"

A cheer erupted on the bridge when Luli opened fire on the Polypheme and the Demetrius. The head of the spaceman wobbled from his new perch as rounds from the coil gun tore the two ships apart. Luli visibly relaxed watching the chunks of starship scatter like a firework burst into the cosmos.

"Thank you for the help, little starman. I need a nap." She yawned and stretched like a cat, "I'm off to bed."

"I'll see that she makes it back, safely," Barney said as he followed her through the hatch.

"Let's get the hell out of here," Jacquie commanded. The coordinates back to the Ankara system were set and ready in the nav system. "And we jump in... three... two... one!"

thirty-one

(Are You) The One That I've Been Waiting for?

The M33 glided through starlit fields, deep into the emptiness of space. The vessel's attitude jets fired from the hull as the ship slowed to a relative stop in an unremarkable stretch of space.

Dr. Wyeth leaned against the back wall and stared daggers into Captain Kaplean's back. He ignored her and stared out the bow port, but as the sensors had indicated, there was nothing to see. Resignation turned his face to stone.

Dr. Wyeth's voice cut through the quiet, "Another dead end? How surprising..."

The Captain interrupted her, "Are you sure these are the coordinates we received from

Baal Shamin?"

"Yes, sir."

"Mr. Cordelan, are you reading anything out there?" asked the Captain.

The Scanner Technician replied, "No sir, still no vessels."

"What about energy readings?" asked Lieutenant Hayley.

"Energy readings?"

A grimace crossed Lieutenant Hayley's face, "Yes. Are you getting energy readings from anything, say a wormhole?"

"Oh." Technician Cordelan reset the ship's scanners and ran a quick and dirty sweep of the area. "Yes, sir! I am picking up residuals from a standard wormhole drive. Hmm... I am also getting some odd energy fluctuations of another type."

"Those look familiar," muttered Ms. Hayley, as she glanced over the readings. "Pull up the scan from the Pequiz system."

Cordelan accessed the records and ran a side by side comparison. "They are similar; they're just on a much smaller scale."

"Then they were definitely here, sir."

Captain Kaplean gave a nod to the Lieutenant, "Confirmation is good, but we still don't know where they are now."

"Um, sir?"

"What is it Mr. Cordelan?"

"The sensors are reading a buildup of those energy fluctuations to the starboard bow."

"Right now?" asked Captain Kaplean.

"Yes, sir."

Lieutenant Hayley felt the hairs on her arms tingle along with an uncontrollable desire to peer out the bow port. She was not alone; the entire bridge crew did the same.

Purple lightning arced outward in a hemispherical formation only to be swallowed by a bluish mist that billowed from the center of it. The mist glowed a faint yellow hue from within before it burned away in a fiery halo of oranges and reds. All of them stood transfixed by the display while a primal fear slowly ground its way into the crew.

"Gunnery Alvarez!" The Captain shouted, "Bring up the weapons systems! Bring the ship around, Grissom, and lay a full broadside into whatever is coming through!"

"Sir! Yes, sir!" the bridge personnel responded. At the sudden violent tilt the sirens triggered and the bridge was bathed in red light. Manny Alvarez manned the weapons systems and set the targeting to the center of the tear in space. His trigger finger ached as he kept the guns locked on the ripples that continued to radiate outward.

The halo parted as the crumpled nose of a ship thrust its way through the center. Waves of pale blue mist undulated along the sides of the vessel. The rip grew until the entire ship tumbled free. Then the tear suddenly shrank and dissipated around the vessel.

Lieutenant Hayley gaped at the

battered freighter, "Is that the Matilda?"

"It most definitely is," Captain Kaplean crowed. "Gunnery! Target her engines and weapons immediately."

"Yes sir," Gunnery Alvarez replied with glee. "You're not getting away from me this time. Rounds away, sir."

Dr. Wyeth grinned fiercely, "You finally prove yourself worthy of your title, Captain."

Multiple explosions shredded the freighter's sublight engines. Simultaneously, small detonations blasted the rail gun assembly into fragments as more rounds burst through the missile tube launches. The shockwaves shook the cargo ship and forced it into a slow spin.

A look of pure satisfaction glowed on the Captain's face. The quarry he had trailed for months was now a fly trapped in his web. "Officer Shimada? Inform Chief Bull to muster four landers with an escort and bring that vessel into my hangar. Have a fully armed detail waiting as well. We will need to crack that ship open."

"Sir! Yes sir!" replied the Communications Officer.

"I have you now," Dr. Wyeth declared in triumph.

***

Rex Leon sighed as he tightly knotted his hands together.

Jon Gray Lang

The flight to the Cat's Eye system had taken longer than expected, but the end result would be the same. In his opinion, the loss in time was worth the cost. A half-smile curled his lip as a much healthier Rosa Keri brought the Independence into orbit around a solitary moon named Sheba.

Rosa's hands released the ship's controls and her face slipped free from the visor, "We are now in orbit, Mr. Leon. Was there anything else you needed from me?"

"Oh no, your entry was impeccable," he replied. "An old resistance trick?"

A smile crossed her face as she vacated the pilot's seat. "From this position, we should resemble a satellite. No one will come looking for us here."

Rho-11 slipped into the pilot's seat. Rosa followed both Rex and Delta into the ready room off the bridge. As the hatch closed, she bumped into a table and gasped in pain.

Delta stood up to help her but was waved away, "Please be careful, Commander Keri. You are better, but you are still healing."

"I appreciate your concern, Captain Delta, but I am not so easily broken."

"No, not in the least," chuckled Mr. Leon.

Delta and Rosa joined in his mirth, even though it did hurt to laugh.

Delta looked around and tentatively asked, "Is more of the tea available?"

Jon Gray Lang

Rex's brightened, "Well, yes and no."

Delta looked bemused, "Yes and no?"

"He means that, yes, there is tea available, but no, we can't have any right now," Rosa smirked at Rex. "Right?"

"Astute as always, Ms. Keri. And also correct," replied Mr. Leon. "Captain Delta, the tea must wait until your latest mission is a success."

Delta nodded in acquiescence, "Of course, Mr. Leon."

Rosa perked up at this, "And what mission is that, Mr. Leon?"

"Why, the time has come, Ms. Keri, to get this revolution started."

thirty-two

The Songs for the Chapter Titles

As it was in my previous books, so it is with this one. All the chapter names are song titles and are part of Ms. Luli Qing's performances. The following songs helped set the mood for the various chapters, and in most cases, I only selected certain versions. If you are curious, here they are:

☐ Be So Happy - Heartless Bastards
☐ Eyes on You - Broken Spirits
☐ Sail On - The Commodores
☐ Darkness - Tarja
☐ La Vie en Rose - Olive Juice
☐ Screaming in Digital - Queensryche
☐ These Boots - Nancy Sinatra
☐ More Whisky - The Caravans
☐ Heart of Oak - Old Folk Song

Jon Gray Lang

- ☐ Freight Train - Old Folk Song
- ☐ Go Get the Ax - Old Folk Song
- ☐ Company Town - Painted Saints
- ☐ Shadowman - Lee Press-On and the Nails
- ☐ The Female Smuggler – Old Folk Song
- ☐ Forever - Hurt
- ☐ High Speed Changer - Orange 9mm
- ☐ God's Gonna Cut You Down - Johnny Cash
- ☐ Le Disko - Shiny Toy Guns
- ☐ F**k It Man - Mellowdrone
- ☐ The Bargain Store - Dolly Parton
- ☐ Mothership Connection (Star Child) - Parliament
- ☐ Good Old Girl - Marian Call
- ☐ Queen of Hearts - Joan Baez
- ☐ Caught Somewhere in Time - Iron Maiden
- ☐ Destroy Everything You Touch - Ladytron
- ☐ Fairies Wear Boots - Black Sabbath
- ☐ Junk Satellite - Man or Astro-Man?
- ☐ These Days - Ane Brune
- ☐ My House Has Wheels - Southern Culture on the Skids
- ☐ Damned if She Do - The Kills
- ☐ (Are You) The One That I've Been Waiting For? – Nick Cave and the Bad Seeds

The title of the book is also a song:
- ☐ Black Matilda - Rum Jacks

Jon Gray Lang

The team is back together and ready to face the future. The Matilda's story continues in Secret Matilda!

Jon Gray Lang

***

About the Author

Jon Gray Lang was born in Australia before being hastily relocated to the United States where he wrote a handful of screenplays, shot a few films, and even threw his hat into the acting ring. But with a life-long love of science fiction, it was only a matter of time before he bit the novel writing bullet and wrote the award-winning five book science fiction series, Saga of a Space Freighter. When he's not typing away at the keyboard, he's busy fighting with rapiers, skiing the Rockies, or banging out tunes on a ukulele... just not all at once... No matter how hard he tries.

Please follow him on:
JonGrayLang.com
facebook.com/JonGrayLang
twitter.com/Jon_Gray_Lang
instagram.com/jongraylang

<<<<>>>>

Jon Gray Lang